"Put this on, then the coat. Lose the leather."

She wanted to argue, but she had some common sense. The sweatshirt and the coat he held in his hand would keep her far warmer than her thin coat ever would. Still, the old leather coat was something of a talisman. It had survived and so had she.

"I've done this before," he said, that quiet sureness she remembered about him threading through those words. Making her waver against the determination not to lean into him. "I can do it again."

She let that break the spell. She'd once thought him infallible magic, but she didn't believe anyone was that anymore. "Don't make promises you don't know you can keep, Jamison. You'll only beat yourself up about it later."

"I'll beat myself up about it either way," he muttered, releasing the zipper. "If you need a break, a rest, a snack, speak up. Best we keep our strength up."

He hefted the pack onto her back again, then pulled two headlamps out of his. He handed her one. "Put it on your head, but leave the light off and stay close to me for as much of the hike as you can." He pulled the small light onto his head, illuminating the space between them.

Then he handed her a gun.

SOUTH DAKOTA SHOWDOWN

Nicole Helm

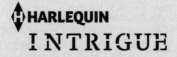

For South Dakota, which was all the inspiration I needed.

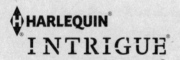

Recycling programs
for this product may
not exist in your area.

ISBN-13: 978-1-335-13636-7

South Dakota Showdown

Copyright © 2020 by Nicole Helm

This edition published by arrangement with Harlequin Books S.A.

For questions and comments about the quality of this book,
please contact us at CustomerService@Harlequin.com.

Harlequin Enterprises ULC
22 Adelaide St. West, 40th Floor
Toronto, Ontario M5H 4E3, Canada
www.Harlequin.com

Printed in U.S.A.

Nicole Helm grew up with her nose in a book and the dream of one day becoming a writer. Luckily, after a few failed career choices, she gets to follow that dream—writing down-to-earth contemporary romance and romantic suspense. From farmers to cowboys, Midwest to *the* West, Nicole writes stories about people finding themselves and finding love in the process. She lives in Missouri with her husband and two sons and dreams of someday owning a barn.

Visit the Author Profile page at Harlequin.com.

CAST OF CHARACTERS

Jamison Wyatt—Sheriff's deputy attached to small town Bonesteel, oldest brother who saved all his younger brothers from his father's gang, Sons of the Badlands.

Liza Dean—Jamison's first girlfriend, whom he saved from the Sons, but she went back to save her sister. Fifteen years later, she needs Jamison's help.

Gigi Dean—Liza's four-year-old half sister, who witnessed her mother's murder then disappeared.

Ace Wyatt—Jamison's father, president of the Sons of the Badlands.

Cody Wyatt—Jamison's youngest brother, who Jamison saved from the Sons at a young age, currently working for a secret group to take down the Sons.

Brady Wyatt—Jamison's brother, a sheriff's deputy.

Gage Wyatt—Brady's twin, also a sheriff's deputy.

Tucker Wyatt—Jamison's brother, detective.

Dev Wyatt—Jamison's brother, lives and works at the Reaves ranch.

Grandma Pauline Reaves—Jamison's grandmother who took in all the boys as they escaped.

Chapter One

Bonesteel, South Dakota, wasn't even a dot on most maps, which was precisely why Jamison Wyatt enjoyed being its attached officer. Though he was officially a deputy with the Valiant County Sheriff's Department, as attached officer his patrol focused on Bonesteel and its small number of residents.

One of six brothers, he wasn't the only Wyatt who acted as an officer of the law—but he was the only man who'd signed up for the job of protecting Bonesteel.

He'd grown up in the dangerous, unforgiving world of a biker gang run by his father. The Sons of the Badlands were a cutthroat group who'd been wreaking havoc on the small communities of South Dakota—just like this one—for decades.

Luckily, Jamison had spent the first five years of his life on his grandmother's ranch before his mother had fully given in to Ace Wyatt and moved them into the fold of the nomadic biker gang.

Through tenacity and grit, Jamison had held on to a belief in right and wrong that his grandmother had instilled in him in those early years. When his mother had given birth to son after son on the inside of the Sons, Jamison had known he would get them out—and he had, one by one—and escaped to their grandmother's ranch situated at the very edge of Valiant County.

It was Jamison's rough childhood in the gang and the immense responsibility he'd placed on himself to get his brothers away from it that had shaped him into a man who took everything perhaps a shade too seriously. Or so his brothers said.

Jamison had no regrets on that score. Seriousness kept people safe. He was old enough now to enjoy the relative quiet of patrolling a small town like Bonesteel. He had no desire to see lawbreaking. He'd seen enough. But he had a deep, abiding desire to make sure everything was *right*.

So, it was odd to be faced with a clear B and E at just a quarter past nine at night on the nearly deserted streets. Maybe if it had been the general store or gas station, he might've understood. But the figure was trying to break into his small office attached to city hall.

It was bold and ridiculous enough to be moderately amusing. Probably a drunk, he thought. Maybe the...woman—yes, it appeared to be a woman—was drunk and looking to sleep it off.

When he did get calls, they were often alcohol related and mostly harmless, as this appeared to be.

Since Jamison was finishing up his normal last patrol for the night, he was on foot. He walked slowly over, keeping his steps light and his body in the shadows. The streets were quiet, having long since been rolled up for the night.

Still, the woman worked on his doorknob. If she was drunk, she was awfully steady. Either way, she didn't look to pose much of a threat.

He stepped out of the shadow. "Typically people who break and enter are better at picking a lock."

The woman stopped what she was doing—but she hadn't jumped or shrieked or even stumbled. She just stilled. Closer now, he could see long dark hair pulled back into a braid, and an oddly familiar beat-up leather jacket that would hardly ward off the chill of a spring night in South Dakota.

Slowly, the woman stood to her full height, back to him. He rested his hand on the butt of his gun, ready for anything, even though he didn't feel particularly threatened by the tall, slender brunette.

The set of her shoulders reminded him of… something he couldn't put his finger on.

Until she turned, slowly, to face him.

He supposed it would have been a shock if he *hadn't* known the perpetrator, but this wasn't a local. It was someone he hadn't laid eyes on in fifteen years. "Liza."

She let out the breath she'd been holding and stepped forward as if it had been days since they'd last seen each other, instead of years. "Thank God, Jamison. You don't know how long I've been trying to find you."

He took her in. Fifteen years should have done

more to change her, but she looked so much the same. Tall, scrappy, with dark, expressive eyes that had always gotten her into trouble with her father. And his own...

Then there was her mouth, which was full and could make a grizzled sailor blush with the creative swearing it could utter.

Once upon a time anyway. This was fifteen years later. Maybe it wasn't half his life, but it was pretty darn close. Liza might want to act like they were old pals, but he wasn't young and easily fooled anymore.

"I need you to come with me," she said, stepping forward, placing her hand on his arm as if they were *more than* old pals as they once had been.

He laughed, not missing how bitter it sounded, and how it made her wince. Undeterred, she scanned the dark around them, fidgety and afraid. When her brown gaze met his, it was with *fear*.

"Do you really think I'd be here if I weren't desperate?" she asked in a tremulous whisper.

For a second, a terrible split second, he believed in that fear and was ready to jump in to help. Then he remembered who he was dealing with. "Desperate? Or working for my father?"

She released his arm as if it was a snake that had bitten her. She even managed to look hurt. Quite the touch.

He'd saved her once. Secreted her out of the eagle eye of her father, who was always in league with his own.

After managing to get his brothers out and to

Grandma Pauline, it had taken some time to get himself out. In part because he wanted his father to know—to really know, once he was gone, that it was he who had gotten the others out.

He'd been eighteen to her sixteen. They'd been friends, though he'd known she was ready and willing to be more. It had felt wrong, like taking advantage. Still, he hadn't been able to leave her behind. Not with her father being as bad as his own. Not with all those feelings buried deep inside.

So, it had taken longer to plan, to work out the route and figure out a time when they'd both be out of the careful watch of their fathers'·men.

He'd done it, too. Grandma hadn't been able to take her in, not with all those wild boys she was raising. But Duke Knight, Grandma's neighbor, had. He and his wife had only been able to have one child of their own despite wanting more, so they'd fostered girls over the years, even adopted some.

They would have adopted Liza. If she'd stayed.

But she'd run off, back to the biker gang, and to everything his father ruled with an iron fist and, sometimes Jamison was quite convinced, pure evil.

Even now he couldn't regret it. Maybe Liza had chosen to go back, but he'd given her the chance. Her choosing to throw it away was her deal. Not his.

"I'm not working for your father," she finally said, vibrating with a loosely controlled anger. The same kind of fury he'd once felt himself.

He'd stopped letting the world make him angry. It had been a hard lesson, but an accomplishment he took great pride in. Or so he had thought, at least before she'd shown up. Instead he could feel that old anger like a geyser getting ready to burst inside him.

But he would control it. He'd built a career and a life on maintaining steady emotions. On being detached enough to get the job done, and engaged enough to care to.

"You'll have to excuse me if I don't take anything a biker gang member says at face value," he managed to utter without too much bitterness tingeing his words. "Not when so many things you said to me once upon a time were lies." Okay, *that* sounded a little bitter.

She shook her head, but she didn't deny it. "You don't understand."

"No, I don't. And I don't want to. Go home, Liza. Back to the life you chose."

"You have no idea what I chose." She cut him off and grabbed his arm again, but this time hard. "Or why I chose it," she added, looking up at him with an emotion he didn't understand. "More important, it doesn't matter. Do you remember Carlee Bright?"

Jamison didn't like to remember anything about his life in that place. His father's camps, or the times they'd take over an entire town and drive people out. Because inflicting pain was Ace Wyatt's currency, and he was a very rich man.

But Jamison remembered the name. "Wasn't she Cody's age?" His youngest brother was nine years his junior, but it felt more like a century considering it was *those* nine years.

"Yes. My dad knocked her up a few years ago."

"Sounds about right, but I don't see why that concerns me. Or you, for that matter."

"Carlee is dead."

"I'm sorry to hear that. If you're looking for police help—"

"Police help? *Police help?* God, Jamison, you never change. A woman is dead, her daughter witnessed it and—"

"How am I supposed to think this isn't a matter for law enforcement?" he interrupted, frustration getting the better of him.

"What are the police going to do about a woman in that gang who is dead? Nothing. You and I both know it."

He didn't respond. He knew the case likely wouldn't have gotten the same kind of attention as another. Certainly not as much as someone who appeared on the grid with no gang association. But it wouldn't be ignored.

Liza would never believe that.

"Is there a body?"

"No. There's a terrified little girl. My half sister. She told me something, Jamison, and now she's disappeared, too. I need help, and I'm not going to get it from the inside."

"But you think you'll get it from me?"

She studied his face for the longest time before she finally smiled, if sadly. "Yeah, I do."

SOMEHOW JAMISON WYATT was almost exactly how Liza remembered. Age had weathered him some, but since he'd always been good-looking, it settled well on him. Lines in the right places, a wariness that made her nerves hum like she was thirteen years old again, watching him as he kept his brothers safe.

That feeling was *just* the same, which was how she knew, no matter how he blustered or accused her of being associated with his father, he'd help. He'd have to help.

Jamison was the one and only reason she believed in goodness. In the midst of all the bad of their child-hoods, when they'd grown up as the direct progeny of some of the worst men in that group, Jamison had still somehow found integrity and honor. By finding it, he'd given it to his brothers and her.

Without him, she never would have seen what the real world looked like outside the Sons of the Bad-lands. She would have never had hope or love. She never would have known homes could be real and safe, and that stealing and lying and always, *always* watching your back was not the only way to live.

The last fifteen years back in the Sons had tried to beat that knowledge out of her, but she'd done what Jamison had always done. She'd gone back to protect her own. She'd failed with her sister, but for four years now she'd been determined to find a way to get her half sister out. Just like Jamison had saved his brothers, Liza was going to save Gigi.

Until she did, until Gigi was safe, she'd stay in the Sons. If she didn't ever get out, she'd always have the satisfaction that she'd worked to help a few other people leave a life that sucked all the good and decent out of them.

She had to find some hope for Gigi and keep it alive. She looked up at the man who still had a good six inches on her, no matter how tall she was for a woman. She didn't have time for the arguments she'd practiced on her way over, not for reasoning, either. She squeezed his arm. "They're going to kill Gigi if I can't find her. If I can't... She's just an innocent bystander."

His jaw worked, his eyes squinting as if trying to hold on to indifference—a familiar move. Years ago she'd run her palm along the hard, chiseled edge of that jaw. She'd been so in awe of him. Too much hero worship and not enough sense.

She couldn't afford to make those mistakes when a little girl depended on her. She had to be strong on her own—to add her strength with his if she ever hoped to save Gigi. She had to believe that if she had a Wyatt brother on her side, she could do this. Rescue Gigi. It was too late for Carlee, but Gigi was still alive.

I hope.

The wave of dizziness that had been plaguing her today came back in full force. She really needed to eat, to get to a place where she could sleep and take care of herself.

"I can take you to the sheriff's department," Jamison said, his voice hard and infused with that cop smugness he'd just been starting to perfect when she'd had to leave the warmth of the Knights' house. "We can take your statement and—"

"I need *you*, Jamison. You know the Sons and you know the law. If you're too busy guarding all this—" she waved a hand to take in the darkened small town, where, at worst, he was taking care of petty crimes "—I'd take the help of one of your brothers. Dev or the twins. They'd know enough. But I need someone who knows Ace and the Sons—enough to be afraid, and how to beat them in spite of that fear."

Though she didn't ask herself why she'd come to him first, when she knew that of all the Wyatt brothers with their various law enforcement jobs, Jamison would be the least likely to forgo protocol.

Except he was the one she needed. If there was an Achilles' heel hidden inside the hard, upstanding man in front of her, it was the desire to save people.

He was silent for far too long. When he spoke, the pain of his words sliced her in two.

"If I could beat Ace, I would have done it already," he said quietly into the dark. A painful rasp made those words *hurt*.

She winced again. She'd known this would be thorny, but she'd also known Jamison was truly her only hope. Any other member of the Sons—man or woman—would be too afraid or too uninterested to help. Even a few sympathetic parties could be a liability in the end.

"When was the last time you tried?" she whispered, the hushed words too loud out here in a town that looked most especially lonely at night. Was Jamison just as lonely?

It was his turn to wince, or maybe take the blow she'd just landed.

He opened his mouth, either to answer or tell her to go, when something exploded, loud and close and painful.

For a second, Liza didn't recognize the sound as that of a gunshot. So much so she was almost surprised when Jamison crashed into her, pushing her underneath him and on to the hardscrabble gravel. His body covered her, warm and heavy.

After a moment—or was it a few moments?—he rolled her on to her back. His hands were on her, she thought, but she couldn't quite feel them. She could see his lips moving, but his voice was garbled.

It was the concern in his dark eyes that worried her. But she was floating away on a cloud of shock she didn't understand. Then radiating pain took her completely under.

Chapter Two

Jamison got Liza in his car, quick as he could. Much as he wanted to chase after the gunman, ascertaining Liza's injuries was first priority. Getting her out of here and to help was second.

Finding the Sons and hurting them would have to come later—for now. Because he had no doubt who'd shot at her.

He laid her out in the back seat of his patrol car. There wasn't enough room, and all his equipment made it all too difficult, but he searched her body for signs of a wound.

He didn't realize he was whispering prayers that she would be all right until he found the injury. Something about his frenzied words and the gash on her leg all coming to a head to remind him to pull himself together.

Taking her to the hospital wasn't the best option with the shooter still out there. A paramedic would insist on a trip to the hospital. So, that was a no go, too.

But his brother was a trained paramedic along with his duties as sheriff's deputy—out here it could be a lifeline. Jamison himself knew a few first aid basics—like bandaging the leg wound, which he did with quick efficiency—but he didn't have the course training and licenses his brother had.

Brady would be able to figure out her loss of consciousness without insisting she be taken to the hospital. Because from what Jamison could tell, the spot on her leg was the only place she'd been hurt, and it wasn't enough for her to pass out for this long.

Debating again, he reached for the radio, then bypassed the idea. Even though it went against his instincts, his ingrained desire to be by the book—to prove he was nothing like Ace Wyatt. He decided this was bigger than the rules.

Just this once.

He picked up his cell and dialed Brady.

"Location?" he barked when Brady answered.

Brady didn't pause or ask why. He simply answered, "Sector A."

Northeast. Good. They could meet in the middle and figure this out. "Meet me on 302nd Avenue in Fuller Junction."

"That's out of my sector, J."

"I'm well aware of where it is. You're off the clock in fifteen."

There was a quiet moment as Jamison shut the doors and climbed into the driver's seat.

"Must be some emergency. Heading that way."

"Same. You'll beat me, but I won't be far behind. Anyone at Grandma's?"

"Just Dev."

"It'll do. Give her a call and tell her we're coming, and to have the first aid kit ready. Yours, too."

Even though Jamison could feel Brady's questions piling up into the silence between them, Brady didn't voice them.

They both hung up and drove toward the meeting point. Jamison had to pay attention to the road in the inky black. He didn't hear a peep from Liza in the back. Just slow, steady breathing. *Thank God.*

That was something at least.

She'd been shot. It wasn't that he didn't believe her story about Carlee Bright. The Sons of the Badlands weren't exactly known for their kind treatment of women. Jamison himself had always wondered about his mother's "drug overdose" when Cody had been a baby. But he hadn't been much more than a child himself. Certainly not adult enough to challenge it.

Sometimes he wondered if that would have mattered.

Carlee Bright wasn't his mother, and the supposed disappearance of Liza's half sister could all be… made-up. Getting shot hardly proved her story. If anything, it proved her connection. She knew too much to be an innocent bystander.

Still, Jamison sped through the dark, not seeing another soul on the streets. He turned onto 302nd, slowed on the gravel road until he spotted Brady's cruiser. Jamison pulled to a stop behind him.

Jamison got out and opened the back seat door. Without a word, Brady immediately examined Liza.

If he recognized her, which surely he did, he didn't mention it.

"She didn't fall or hit her head?"

"Not that I saw."

Brady nodded toward the driver's seat. "She could have just passed out from shock. Let's get her to the ranch. I need more space and more light."

But they both knew a woman who'd grown up in a biker gang wasn't exactly gun-shy. She'd seen way worse than this kind of wound.

"You sure you want to take her to Grandma's? Hospital would be…safer," Brady said carefully.

Too carefully. As if he thought Jamison was still hung up on a woman he hadn't seen in fifteen years and had gotten over years ago. *Years* and years ago. This was about the Sons, and it was about keeping someone safe. He'd dedicated his life to keeping strangers safe. Why wouldn't he keep Liza safe, too? It was just…his job. "I'll meet you at the ranch."

Brady nodded and strode back to his car.

They drove, and occasionally Liza would come to, move around a bit, ask where she was. Jamison tried to keep her talking, but she faded in and out. It worried him, even as the fact she kept waking up eased some of his fears.

Finally, he turned off onto the unmarked gravel road that would twist through the rolling hills of the South Dakota ranch and farmland. Then, behind the hills, home.

There was a light on outside the old farmhouse— there always ways. Pauline Reaves was used to visitors at all times of night. She kept her doors open, her windows homey and a variety of weapons within easy reach should any of the *bad* element ever show up at her door.

It was home, even if he'd spent most of his adolescence in various Sons of the Badlands camps. This house with its piecemeal layout, thanks to being over a century old and needing all sorts of additions and modern conveniences, was his heart and soul.

By the time he reached the end of the gravel road and pushed the car into Park, Grandma Pauline was at the door. Jamison opened the back door of his cruiser and Liza blinked at him.

"Come on now."

She closed her eyes and took a deep breath before pushing herself out of the back seat. She was on her feet a second before she swayed, so Jamison scooped her up into his arms and started marching toward the house—Brady closing the door for him and following.

Dev's two ranch dogs pranced at their feet but had been trained not to bark at a Wyatt or a Knight. They whimpered excitedly instead, obviously hoping to be petted.

Brady obliged since Jamison had his hands full.

"I can walk," Liza said, attempting outrage, though it was weak at best.

"No, you can't."

She was too light by half, and her clothes fairly hung off her—except for that too-thin leather coat he did indeed remember from fifteen plus years ago.

He strode through the front door and Grandma

didn't blink an eye as her eldest grandson carried in a bleeding, unsteady ex-girlfriend, followed by another grandson.

Both in uniform.

Brady closed the door, the dogs knowing better than to enter here, where they'd have to trot through Grandma's kitchen. Grandma Pauline did not allow such things.

"Kitchen," she instructed. "Best light."

As if they didn't already know. It might not be so commonplace these days, but once upon a time the Wyatt brothers had gotten into their share of scrapes and had been patched up in Grandma's kitchen.

Dev was already there, with one of Grandma's "medical" sheets laid out over the kitchen table.

He raised an eyebrow at Liza but otherwise didn't say anything. Not all that uncommon for Dev. But even though he didn't speak, his disapproval came off him in waves.

Jamison sat Liza down on the table. "Believe me now?" she asked archly, before wincing as she moved the leg that had been shot.

Jamison chose to follow Dev's example and kept silent.

"Let's have a look," Brady offered, approaching the table. He pulled back the bandage and examined the wound under better light. Grandma set a washcloth and small basin of water next to him—the first aid kit already opened and laid out.

Brady ripped the hole in her jeans so he had a large enough space to work. He cleaned out the wound, Grandma handing Liza an over-the-counter painkiller and a glass of water when she hissed out a breath.

"Have any idea why you might have passed out?" Brady asked, his voice calm and pleasant. "Recent head wound? Any other injuries?"

Liza shook her head.

"Pregnant?"

"No," she said flatly, and her gaze stayed resolutely on where Brady worked on her thigh.

"When was the last time you ate, girl?" Grandma demanded.

Liza ran a shaky hand through her hair as Brady rebandaged the wound. "I don't…"

"Girl needs a meal," Grandma said firmly, already moving for the refrigerator.

"Broth, Grandma," Brady ordered.

At Grandma's harrumph, Jamison knew Liza wouldn't just be getting broth.

The woman in question looked around the kitchen from her seat atop the table and tried to smile, but it frayed. "Didn't expect half the Wyatt crew at my beck and call."

"Don't get shot, then," Dev replied sharply.

"I'm no doctor," Brady said, interrupting the back-and-forth, though his comment made both Jamison and Dev shift because Brady certainly would have made a good physician. But an elderly woman raising six boys in the middle of nowhere, South Dakota, didn't have the kind of resources to make that happen.

So, Brady had become a paramedic and a cop, and he was excellent at both, but the two older brothers often wondered what if…?

"My guess would be the loss of consciousness came from a combination of a lack of food and shock. There aren't any other symptoms that point to anything more going on. Get enough food in her, keep the bandage clean, she should be fine."

"*She* is sitting right here."

"That she is," Brady replied with a patient smile. "You're going to want to take it easy. *And* you're going to want to tell us why someone's shooting at you."

She leveled Jamison with a haughty look. "I guess your brother can explain it."

Jamison held her stare. "Liza thinks her father murdered Carlee Bright, and that her half sister, who witnessed it, has been kidnapped and is in mortal danger. Like Liza herself apparently is."

THE WAY JAMISON so neutrally delivered the details of her situation made her shiver. She instantly had a blanket draped over her shoulders, thanks to Brady.

Silence descended over the kitchen, except for the sounds of Pauline puttering at the stove.

"How do you know Carlee is dead?" Jamison asked.

"Now you're interested?" she retorted. She felt shaky and off-kilter and her leg throbbed where the bullet had—thank God—just grazed her.

"I wouldn't go so far as to say interested. Obviously

you're mixed up with something involving the Sons," he said, gesturing toward her torn jeans and the bandage. "I certainly wouldn't be surprised if your father killed Carlee. I'm having a harder time imagining he'd harm his own daughter. If only because you're still alive. He's had ample time and reason to kill you."

She glanced at the three Wyatt brothers standing next to each other. Each with arms crossed over broad chests. They had the physical look of their father—big men, hard men. Dark hair and eyes that ranged from brown to green. Their jaws were chiseled, their mouths all in firm disapproval.

All had aged, Dev most especially. He didn't just look weathered, he looked…beaten. She knew any questions about his limp would be met with stony silence.

Just like she knew the Wyatt boys had souls, thanks to the woman bustling around her now. Ace had no soul, Liza knew. His sons had been born or become good men in spite of it.

"Gigi is four years old," Liza said, trying very hard to find the balance between overwrought and detached. If she was too emotional, they would dismiss her. If she wasn't emotional enough, they'd think she was some kind of plant sent by Ace. "She *saw* my father kill Carlee."

"Why would the Sons of the Badlands be scared about what a four-year-old girl says?" Jamison returned. "Surely there are enough kids running around those camps who've seen as much. And they have no recourse. There's no one to tell who would do anything about it."

"She told me, Jamison," Liza said, trying to eradicate the lump in her throat. "She told me. The next day she was gone. I… Someone's been following me ever since. They know I know and now someone's shot me. After I approached you."

"Aren't you one of them?" Dev returned, as hard if not harder than Jamison.

One of them. Years ago Pauline would have demanded an apology out of Dev, defended Liza to anyone that her ties to the Sons of the Badlands were severed.

But that was just another thing she'd lost when she'd gone back to them—Pauline's trust. There was no point being sad about it. She was here for Gigi, not herself.

"Regardless, if they really thought you knew something you'd already be dead," Jamison said, his voice flat and his eyes hard.

He was right, which scared her more than anything, but it also crystallized something about Jamison for her. If he didn't want to help her, she wouldn't be here. He would have taken her to the hospital. Not home.

He might put on the gruff, aloof cop act, but he'd brought her *home*. To his grandma's. Because even if she'd only had four years over at the Knights' ranch, Grandma Pauline had been hers, just like Duke and Eva Knight had been something like parents.

But she hadn't been able to stay with them. When

Jamison had convinced her to escape the Sons with him, when he'd given her this home and *family*, she'd thought she could do it. She'd been sure she could accept her sister was a lost cause.

The more she'd been given at the Knights', the guiltier she'd felt that her sister was still in that awful place. The more she'd seen Jamison's brothers thrive—because he'd saved them before he'd saved himself—the harder it had been to live with herself.

She'd had to leave the Knights and go back to the Sons, to try to save Marci. In the end, it *had* been a lost cause. Marci didn't want to leave, didn't want to see the good in the world.

But Gigi was only four. She had a chance at a real life. A safe, good life. So, Liza had given up on one sister and focused on another.

Now she had no one and nothing—here, where she'd once been loved. But that didn't mean she couldn't use what she knew to get Jamison's help.

"I just need to find Gigi, and I can't do it on my own. You know I can't ask for help in that place."

"And you know I can't help you *in* that place."

She closed her eyes against that simple truth. She just kept hoping… No. She didn't have time to hope. Gigi's life was at stake.

"One of you will help me," she said. "You know too much what it's like to be a kid in that place. You know what it's like to watch horrors, to lose your mother and only have an awful, scary father left. One of you has to help me. You know it."

No one said anything for the longest time. Pauline

handed her a warm mug of broth and a plate with a sandwich on it.

Liza looked at the elderly woman handing her food and wanted to break down and cry, offer apologies and beg for forgiveness.

But fifteen years was too long, and she had bigger issues at hand.

Eventually Brady turned to face Jamison.

"You're still on duty," he said, keeping his voice low as if she wouldn't be able to hear it.

Jamison's jaw tensed.

"I'll take your car back. Take your place till shift change. If something goes down, it'll be both our butts in a sling, but I'll do it."

Jamison only nodded. Brady gave her one last enigmatic look, kissed his grandmother on the cheek, then left the kitchen.

Still, Jamison didn't say anything. No one offered to help. They maintained their silence and Liza tried to ignore panic. She had to eat, that much was for sure. Too many days trying to keep out of reach of the Sons, while also trying to find Gigi, had left her with almost no supplies and far, far too long between meals.

But it was hard to eat when your stomach was twisted in awful knots. When every move felt like one that might end Gigi's life, or her own.

She swallowed some broth, doing everything she could not to cry.

"You boys go make up two rooms," Pauline ordered.

Dev and Jamison looked like they wanted to

argue, but Liza knew they wouldn't. Not with Grandma Pauline.

They turned and left the kitchen, leaving Liza alone with her food and the woman she'd looked up to as a teenager.

"You eat that all up before I let you out of my sight, you hear?"

Liza nodded, her vision wavering. This time not from exhaustion or losing consciousness, she didn't think, but because her eyes were full of tears.

"None of that now, girl. You've got a life to save. How are you going to do it?"

"I don't know," Liza whispered. "If Jamison won't help me, I don't know what I'll do." She wouldn't have said that aloud to anyone else, but she knew Pauline would keep her shameful weakness a secret.

In her no-fuss way Pauline used a dish towel to wipe the tears off Liza's cheeks. She picked up the sandwich herself and held it out to Liza until she accepted it and took a bite.

"Jamison will help you. Stomp around a bit and put on the manly act, but he'll help. Won't be able to stop himself." Pauline studied her. "But you can't let that stubborn pride of yours get in the way, girl. And he can't let his."

All Liza could think was: *good luck with that*.

Chapter Three

"I don't like it." Dev leaned more to the right than the left, because his left leg was bad. A gift from Ace when Dev had been a young cop determined to take their father down.

Each of the Wyatt boys had learned, in their own way, that you didn't take the Sons down without getting hurt.

None of them had let their past experiences sway them completely, but each of their obsessions had been stilted by Dev's near-death encounter ten years ago. Jamison had found it necessary to give up on revenge in the face of his brother almost dying.

Jamison sighed. "What *do* you like, Dev?"

He didn't answer that question. "She can't be here."

"And yet, here she is." Jamison hadn't thought it through, bringing her here, but there was no other option. He knew what it meant for himself, for his brothers. It was getting pulled back in when they'd all silently agreed to stay out.

No matter all those old feelings and promises, this felt something like inevitable.

They'd escaped the Sons of the Badlands, but their father still existed, still ran a group full of criminals, no matter how many of his biological sons had gone into law enforcement.

"You're not just bringing trouble home, you're bringing it to the Knights' doorstep, as well."

That poked at Jamison, but he had to believe he could handle it. "She seems fine. We'll get out of here in the morning."

"We?"

Jamison stood from where he'd made up the bed for Liza—perfectly because he knew Grandma would still box his ears if he didn't do the chore correctly.

"Do you remember what it was like to be four years old in that place?"

Dev was quiet for a moment, then shrugged and didn't meet Jamison's gaze. "I didn't know any better."

"You know you did. And if that little girl saw something—"

"And if that not-so-little girl is BS-ing you, then what? You wind up dead?"

"I can see through Liza's BS." God, he hoped he was older and wiser than he'd been at twenty-two.

Dev laughed coldly. "Since when? You thought you two were going to get married and be the example for any kid stuck in that hellhole. A fairy tale told to dirty faces so they could believe they'd escape someday. Then she ditched you. For them."

It stung, because the truth could, but Jamison was too old to get riled up about his brother's barbs.

"I've got too many what-ifs, brother. I can't take on another. I'll be careful, but I've got to help her find this little girl."

Which was enough of an emotional truth for Dev not to say another word. They moved to the room across the hall, which had been the room Jamison and Dev had shared years and years ago. Now, Dev slept downstairs in the mudroom converted to bedroom.

Taking the stairs every day was too hard on his leg. Especially in the morning, when it was stiff from sleep.

"You'll have to be careful. You can't trust her. No matter what memories she stirs up."

"I don't trust her," Jamison said, maybe a pinch too loudly. Because his instincts when it came to Liza were a mess, that was for sure. But he knew it. If you could identify a problem, you could address it. So, there'd be no trust. He'd follow his own instincts and beliefs and—

"Good to know."

They both looked up to find Liza in the doorway. Jamison didn't feel particularly guilty—it was something he would have said to her face. But something about how pale she was and the sleeve of saltines in her hand poked at him.

He stood stiffly. "Your room is across the hall."

She glanced behind her, then smirked. "Lucky me."

She walked over to her room, favoring the leg that hadn't been shot.

"Watch yourself, J. She is nothing but trouble. I can guarantee it." Then Dev did his own limping out of the room.

Jamison let himself breathe in and then out a few calming times. Liza was no doubt trouble, always had been, but that didn't mean he could ignore a four-year-old stuck in a bad situation.

She was hardly the only little girl in a bad situation associated with the Sons, or the world at large, for that matter. As a cop Jamison had come to accept that he *couldn't* help everyone, but that he should certainly try to help whoever he could.

He opened the dresser drawers in his old room until he found what he wanted. He walked across the hall, knocked perfunctorily before opening the door.

She swore at him, then stood there glaring.

She'd taken off the ripped jeans, which had messed with the bandage. Now she stood only in a long-sleeved T-shirt and her underwear. Her legs were as long and mesmerizing as he remembered, and he stared a beat too long.

But that didn't mean he didn't know how to recover. He gestured at the bandage. "Need help?"

"Yeah. Why don't you put your hands on me while I'm half-naked?"

He raised his gaze to meet hers. "Worried you can't control yourself around me, darling?"

She scoffed, but the corner of her mouth kicked up with *some* humor. "Fine. Help."

He placed the map on the bed and then crouched down by her leg, refitting the bandage and smoothing the tape over. It required touching warm skin and a copious amount of control not to remember all the times he'd touched her for completely romantic reasons.

They'd been different people way back then—smooth skin or not.

He stood and didn't dare look at her face. "Let's talk logistics."

"God, that's so hot," she said dryly.

He sent her a look, saw her pulling her jeans back on and shook his head. "Wait."

She frowned, good leg in one leg of the jeans. "Huh?"

He strode out of the room again, went rummaging through his old drawers, found an old pair of gym shorts and returned to her room. "Here." He tossed them at her.

She caught them and studied them, then shrugged and dropped the jeans. She slipped the shorts on, tying the drawstring tight. They landed below her knees, although she was a tall woman herself. But it was hardly a good idea to be wearing shorts on a cold early-spring night in a rickety old farmhouse.

"Now, it's not near warm enough up here for that, so why don't you crawl under the covers?"

"You're really going to have to stop coming on to me, Jamison."

"Ha ha. Get in bed."

She fluttered her eyelashes at him as she slid under the covers, trying—and failing—to cover up the wince of pain as she presumably laid her weight a little too hard on her wound.

He picked up the map he'd brought in and smoothed it out over her lap. "Where?"

Her hesitation spoke volumes and reminded him of all the ways she'd once fooled him.

And never would again.

"You and your cop buddies can't go in there guns blazing. Gigi won't be the only one hurt."

"Do you see a slew of my 'cop buddies' crowding in here, Liza? Or is it just you and me?"

"It's complicated. Surely you understand that."

"Either you can tell me where the main camp is and I see what I can do to help Gigi, or you sleep off your gunshot wound and fend for yourself tomorrow in the morning."

She looked up at him, her dark eyes too direct and assessing. As if she still knew him, understood him. "You'd love to believe you're that tough, wouldn't you?"

"Try me."

LIZA LOOKED AT the paper map—of all things—of South Dakota spread out on her lap. She knew exactly what he wanted to know, and that she had all the information he desired. Except she didn't hesitate for the reasons he thought.

Jamison saw dealings with the Sons as black-and-white. He believed you were with them or against them—he'd had too many years winning against them as an officer of the law. He was a man after all, and it was so easy to see the world as with you or against you when you held the power.

But Liza had lost in that world, and losers had a much more complicated view of things.

She was worried about Gigi, about how to get to her. She was worried about *anyone* who risked their life to help her—because lives *were* on the line.

But specifically she worried about involving Jamison.

She knew Ace Wyatt would someday decide to exact revenge against his sons. He had plans, but he was a patient man. He'd go after them when they least expected it, when Ace most needed it. She knew Ace was always looking for that perfect moment to make it poetic justice or divine revenge or whatever went on in his head.

She didn't want to send Jamison riding into Sons territory knowing it could be the shot that started a war.

You know he's your only chance or you wouldn't have come here. Besides, you think Ace Wyatt doesn't know exactly where you are?

She looked up at Jamison—now in immediate danger because of her. She'd been shot. Of course Ace, or even her own father, had sent someone to do that. If either had pulled the trigger, she knew damn well she'd be dead.

The shot was meant to be a warning. Furthermore,

whoever had shot her would have followed her. Jamison was involved now, whether he chose to be or not.

Guilt swamped her. She looked down at the map, surprised to find tears clouding her vision. She didn't think she had tears left anymore. "I'm sorry," she whispered.

"There are a lot of things you could be sorry for, Liza. I'm afraid you'll have to be more specific."

She would never be sorry for leaving the Knights to go back to the Sons all those years ago, but she didn't think telling him that in the moment would do any good for either of them. "I'm sorry for this, because they'll know you're involved, even if you decide not to be. Whatever happens, this will be the start of something. I didn't think that through."

He held her gaze for a long time. "Every beginning has an end, Liza." He pointed at the map. "Now. Where?"

Knowing it couldn't possibly end well, but that it was Gigi's only chance to survive, Liza pointed. "Here. They've taken over Flynn."

Jamison's expression hardened. "Flynn."

"You know it?"

"That's where dear old Dad was born, where his parents abandoned him. Where he took us out and taught us to be men. I don't think that's a coincidence he's settled down there right now, Liza. Whatever war you're worried about starting—Ace already beat you to it."

Chapter Four

Jamison didn't sleep much. Brady had finished off his shift without anything cropping up, and Jamison had done the unthinkable and called in to his superior officer, requesting to use all of his vacation time.

He'd built up quite a lot. There'd been questions, hemming and hawing, but in the end, Sheriff Sneef couldn't deny Jamison deserved a "vacation."

Yeah, some vacation.

Grandma came into the kitchen through the back porch. He heard the squeak of the door, the whimper of the dogs left outside, then the stomp of her boots against the rug before she bustled into the kitchen, a basket with a few eggs cradled inside on her arm.

"You're up, then."

There was just a *hint* of disapproval in her tone, but it was hard to wake up early enough to suit Grandma.

No doubt Dev was already out with the cows, grumbling over the fact his ranch hand was Sarah Pleasant, one of the Knights' foster girls. Not a girl anymore, and splitting her time helping her guardian on his ranch and wounded Dev on his.

Because life at the ranch went on no matter what was going on with Ace and the Sons. Whether you'd lost your wife to cancer like Duke had, or you'd lost full function of your body after a run-in with Ace like Dev had.

"We'll be out of your hair soon. I'd like Liza to get a good breakfast in first."

Grandma simply made a noise of assent as she pulled out a pan. She went about breakfast preparations as if everything was fine.

Jamison wished he believed that could be true. Bringing Liza here last night had brought Grandma into the thick of things. It wasn't the first time, and probably wouldn't be the last, but it was hard not to feel guilty about it.

She'd never asked for this. It was hardly her fault her only child had been taken in by the likes of Ace Wyatt. Certainly not her lot in life to take care of their six rowdy, traumatized boys.

But she'd done it. Now she was creeping up on eighty, and he could see the weight of the Wyatt world on her shoulders. It was a burden she'd taken on, and she'd done it without a complaint.

"You'll need to be on watch," he said as blandly as he could manage. Because any true expression of worry would be offensive to her, any command would make her bristle and sure to do the opposite.

"I'm always on watch." She turned from the stove

and studied him in that way of hers. "Don't doubt yourself. Not on this."

It was no surprise Grandma Pauline could see right through him, but that didn't ease his concern. "It's complicated."

"The right thing usually is, Jamison," she said, turning back to her meal preparation.

Jamison had been attempting to do the right thing his whole life. Getting there—like Grandma said—was rarely simple.

Liza walked into the kitchen. She looked like she'd had a rough night. Grandma immediately handed her a glass of water and some over-the-counter pills for pain.

"Thanks, Pauline."

"Sit. Breakfast will be just a bit."

Liza slid into the chair farthest from him. Which would have been great if they weren't about to embark on a dangerous mission together. Truth be told, he'd rather leave her behind, especially with her injuries.

But she knew what they were looking for better than he did.

Dev's warning sat in his gut. He couldn't ignore the possibility Liza had been sent. That this was an elaborate scheme to get him on his father's territory.

Jamison might have washed his hands of the Sons years ago, but he'd always known his father wasn't the kind of man to let that stand. Maybe Jamison had gotten a little complacent when his father hadn't instigated any attacks since Dev's run-in ten years ago. Maybe Jamison had begun to hope escape was really enough.

But that didn't mean he was surprised at being drawn back in.

Whatever parts of the truth Liza was telling him, Jamison did believe a little girl was in danger. Which meant he needed Liza if he was going to be able to find Gigi. Liza knew a lot more than she was telling him, he was sure, and she had far more insider knowledge of the Sons' recent movements than he did.

They'd have to work together.

"I'm surprised there aren't reinforcements," Liza offered into the quiet kitchen.

"Brady, Tucker and Gage all have jobs, Liza. Ones they can't leave at a whim."

"So, I *did* come to the right brother."

"I had vacation time to take, so I took it. You're welcome, by the way."

"What about Cody? You didn't include him in your laundry list of important men with important things to do."

Jamison's entire adult life was dealing with people who questioned and sometimes even challenged his authority—starting with being saddled with five brothers who had smart mouths and no compunction trying to get under his skin. He should be quite adept at handling Liza's little barbs.

Or so he told himself.

"Cody isn't any of your concern."

"Don't tell me one of the Wyatt brothers isn't quite

so chummy with the rest. What? The baby Wyatt run away?"

"That'll be enough," Grandma said in that quiet way of hers that was scarier than when she was threatening a man with a wooden spoon to the head.

She slid a plate in front of Liza, then Jamison. Both were loaded with bacon and eggs and biscuits. Age had slowed her down some, but it hadn't stopped her from doing a darn thing.

"Jamison, I've packed up quite a few provisions. Obviously, you'll want to take your camping supplies just in case. Still, I'll put together some linens."

"I can—"

It only took a very carefully raised eyebrow for Jamison to swallow the rest of his words. Heaven forbid he try to patronize his grandmother with assistance.

She didn't want to be treated like an "old lady." It was hard to learn the balance between truly helping her and jabbing at her pride.

"I see things haven't changed around here," Liza said once Grandma had left the kitchen.

Jamison wished that were true. But things had changed. Dev's injuries. Cody's evasiveness about his job that kept him far away from the ranch. The middle lot hadn't changed much and all worked for Valiant County. Gage enjoyed pretending he was a happy-go-lucky sheriff's deputy, his twin, Brady, taking on a more serious outlook with the same job, while Tucker's detachment to the detective bureau kept him busy and satisfied—supposedly.

But Jamison wondered if they'd just gotten better at hiding their scars as adults.

A concern and a worry for another day. He ate the breakfast Grandma had set in front of him. Liza did as well, without any more commentary. Thank God.

She scraped her plate clean, which comforted Jamison some. He took their plates to the sink once they were both done and didn't miss the way she watched him. She was here because she thought he was the only one who could help her—not because she necessarily *wanted* his help.

Wasn't that always the way with her?

As long as he remembered that, as long as he didn't get sucked into old memories, this would be fine.

He took Liza outside to help pack up the truck. Grandma's truck was a nondescript Ford that would suit him well. Brady and Gage would get Jamison's truck out to the ranch for Grandma to use later today.

"This is a lot," Liza said, sounding something between wary and exhausted as he crammed another cooler into the bed along with all his camping supplies. She crouched nearby, petting the dogs.

"We don't know what we'll need or for how long, and I don't want you passing out on me again."

She didn't smirk or even make a snotty comeback like he'd hoped—no, not hoped—expected. There could be nothing to do with hope when it came to Liza.

She stood and hugged herself instead, looking

out at the endless rolling landscape of the ranch. "They're going to know we're coming."

There was a rawness to that statement he simply couldn't let affect him. "I know it's been a while, but surely you know me better than to think I don't understand that."

"You can't underestimate them."

Jamison looked over at Dev limping from the barn, and the small figure that was Sarah. Dev started walking toward them, and Sarah toward the house. The dogs raced to Dev. It made a nice picture, all in all, but his brother's limp stuck in his craw.

No, he'd never underestimate his father or the Sons again.

LIZA DIDN'T MISS the look Jamison gave his brother. She was definitely missing pieces of that story. Part of her wanted to ask, wanted to dig. The Wyatt brothers and their grandmother still felt like family even if she'd cut them off fifteen years ago.

Worse, so much worse than that feeling was the fact beyond Dev were rolling fields. Behind those hills was the Knight place.

Was Duke still running his cattle, laughing uproariously at himself and his over-the-top stories? Were her foster sisters from those beautiful few years she'd spent under their roof still there? Or had they built beautiful lives of their own?

Did they all hate her?

"I'd say you could stop by, but I don't want to drag Duke and the girls into this."

Liza swallowed, looking away from Sarah's far-off form and the only true home she'd ever had. "No, I don't, either." She didn't want to ask which girls. Leaving meant she'd learned that no information was better than some and knowing she couldn't be part of it.

"Sarah and Rachel still live on the ranch. Cecilia lives on the reservation—she's tribal police now. Felicity's a park ranger over at Badlands."

She didn't want to ask, but he'd started it. "What about Nina?"

Jamison shrugged. "She left."

"Left… How?"

"Do you really want to know, Liza? Because, by my count, the past fifteen years were yours for the knowing."

It hurt because it was true, and because it was true she didn't know what to say. But Dev approached, looking stormy and grumpy—which was different from the eager, determined teenager she remembered.

Maybe some things *had* changed.

"Heading out?"

"Looks like. Grandma was getting together a few more things. I'll be in touch."

Dev nodded, then turned his attention to her. Disapproval was etched into every line on his face, and none of it was softened by the beard that hid most of his mouth. "Watch your back, brother," he said, though he said the words while looking at her.

She didn't bother to plead her case to Dev, or to

Jamison, for that matter. She'd broken their trust, knowing full well how slow trust was gained when it came to the Wyatts. Whatever they wanted to lay at her feet was fine, as long as they found Gigi.

Pauline came out with another load of who knew what. Liza felt like they were packing for a covered wagon trip across the prairie. She'd gotten by on next to nothing the past few days. Of course she'd ended up shot and unconscious.

Jamison said his goodbyes, giving strict instructions to be contacted if anything fishy happened at the ranch. Then they were loaded up in Pauline's truck and driving away from the ranch.

Liza watched the gorgeous scenery go by. Spring was trying to get ahold of the land. There were touches of green peeking through just about every rolling brown hill. The scarce few bare trees they drove by were softening with buds.

Jamison drove west, which was right where the Sons were camped for the time being. It put Liza on considerable edge. Maybe he was just going to deliver her back to the Sons and be done with her.

But no. Jamison wouldn't willingly go into Sons territory. Certainly not for her. "Where exactly are we going?" she asked when she couldn't stand another minute of silence.

"Not directly to Flynn if that's what you're worried about."

She wasn't sure what she was worried about. Everything, maybe. She'd come to Jamison because he was the only one who could help, but that didn't mean she wouldn't doubt his methods. He was a *cop* now. He wouldn't be breaking any laws to bring her sister to safety.

It was about two hours between Flynn and Pauline's ranch, and they'd already been going for over an hour. Jamison said they weren't going directly to Flynn, but it sure felt like they were.

Liza pressed her forehead against the passenger window. Out of the corner of her eyes she saw a flash and she looked in the rearview mirror. Her entire body went cold. "Right about now I'm worried about the tail we've got," she said, her throat tight with fear.

Jamison grinned, just like he'd done when they were younger. Irritatingly, her stomach did the same stupid swoop it had always done back then, too.

"I'm not," he offered, then without any warning punched the gas and sped off the road.

Chapter Five

Jamison wouldn't admit to anyone there was an excitement in all this that he'd missed. A thrill he'd thought he'd left behind when he'd become a cop.

But taking the truck over the edge of the road, slamming down the gas pedal a little too hard as they sped over the hills, turning too tight around rock formations, it filled him with a dark satisfaction he hadn't allowed himself to feel in a long time.

He slid a quick glance at Liza. Her expression vacillated between worry as she looked behind them, and that wicked smile he remembered. She'd always been fueled by danger—even more than him.

But this wasn't the old days, a fact he had a bad feeling he was going to have to remind himself of over and over.

There wasn't much cover, even as they got closer to the landscape that dipped and cratered with soaring stone ridges. The closer they got, the more impossible it would become to drive quickly or evade their pursuer.

"All right. Hold on."

He did a tight 180. Liza screeched—out of fear or delight it was hard to tell—but the truck held and Jamison sped directly toward their tail. He passed them, a pinch too close, their door mirrors crashing into each other and splintering off.

Jamison swore. "Grandma's going to kill me for that," he muttered, speeding back to the highway, gaining enough distance from their tail to get back on the road and make it to the turnoff he wanted without being seen.

Liza kept watching out the back window as Jamison maneuvered down a gravel side road that would take him where he wanted to go.

"It's not going to be that easy."

"No. I'd wager that's only the beginning. But the one thing we've got going for us is they're not going to kill us."

"How do you know that?"

"Because if anyone in that group is going to kill us, it's going to be our fathers. That's one thing they're not going to send their goons to do. Or we'd have been dead a long time ago."

"Isn't that even the tiniest bit depressing to you?"

"If a man like my father wants to kill me, I figure I've made a pretty good life for myself."

"Policing some Podunk town in the middle of no-where."

The insult didn't bother him. He wouldn't let it. He hadn't built his adult life to impress his ex-girlfriend who'd betrayed him once upon a time. So, he replied to her bland statement lightly, confidently,

"Keeping the people of a small, tight-knit community safe from the likes of my father. It works for me."

"Some of us choose to protect the people inside from the likes of your father."

"Is that what you thought you were doing when you left, Liza? Protecting the people who willingly follow our fathers around—and willingly hurt and kill people in their paths?"

"Children don't have a choice, Jamison. You should know that better than anyone else."

He didn't have a response for that. He couldn't—*wouldn't*—believe she'd gone back to the Sons all those years ago to protect children when she'd still practically been a child. Or that she wouldn't have tried to explain that to him instead of disappearing in the middle of the night, making them all fear the worst.

He opened his mouth to say *that*, to ask her if she had any idea what she'd put all of them through those first few days. How worried sick the Knights and their girls had been, how he and his brothers had mounted a search-and-attack plan.

Until Grandma had stated the obvious. Clearly, Liza had left of her own accord.

Ancient history. Let it go.

He took the next turn a little too quickly considering he was almost certain they'd lost the tail. He followed this dirt road, backtracking toward Bonesteel, then taking a few paved roads back to the highway farther west.

"They'll still know where we're going," Liza said, not bothering to hide her disgust.

"But they won't know how. Or when. Do you think Gigi is in Flynn?"

"I'm not sure. I couldn't find her, but that doesn't mean anything. Dad was around the whole time, so she's either in Flynn, or someone's taken her away and is waiting for Dad."

"The second is more likely if you couldn't find her." Which made things more difficult, but not impossible.

She closed her eyes as if that truth hurt. "Yeah."

"So, where are the Sons holding ancillary camps right now?"

"I don't know, Jamison. I was hardly top of the food chain."

"You couldn't have been that low if you were there."

She shook her head. "You never, ever once understood that it's different for women in there. When you're property to be traded around, no one needs revenge on you. Being there is revenge enough."

Maybe there was a truth to that, but it didn't negate his truth, either. "The Sons don't let anything live that doesn't have use to them."

"And yet here you are, alive and well. What use do you serve, Jamison?"

It was pointless to try to get through to her. And she was wrong. He'd understood he had a different place in the Sons than she did when they were still stuck there. Why did she think he'd risked his life to get her out?

But with or without her cooperation he could make some educated guesses. Luckily, he knew the area around Flynn well. When he'd been growing up, the Sons had had two main camps—one directly in the Badlands, though outside the park, and another closer to Bonesteel. Flynn had been the middle ground, and Dad's special place. He'd called it sentimental, but Jamison had known better than that.

Flynn was where Ace Wyatt had taken his sons when he wanted to hurt them. Warp them and mold them into the kind of man Ace was.

The fact Ace had never been able to do it was probably his biggest and only regret. Which was why Jamison had known, no matter how he'd hoped otherwise, that he walked through this life with a target on his chest.

Dad wouldn't die until he exacted revenge on his sons for refusing to be broken. Ace had built his gang and his power on his control, though. He didn't need death and revenge immediately. He wanted it to hurt. He wanted it to *mean* something.

Letting his children build lives, only to take them away, was exactly the kind of thing Ace got off on.

Jamison glanced at Liza. There was true fear there—for Gigi. But this could still be a trap. For all he knew, his father or hers could have demanded his head for Gigi's. He wouldn't put it past any of them, and he could hardly blame Liza for using him to save her sister.

"You know, if they sent you here under the guise of some kind of trade, it's not going to end well."

She laughed. Bitterly. "I know you don't know me at all, and, sure, I'd love to trade your life for my sister's, but they didn't ask. Even if they had, I'd know better than to make a deal with the devil. The devil always wins, and I will not let Gigi lose."

She was vehement and angry, and he wished that didn't make him believe her. He wished it could remind him to harden himself against her. But when it came to Liza, wishes had never come true.

"If we save her—get her out and safe, truly safe, you won't be able to go back. Not ever."

She turned her head to meet his gaze. Her dark eyes were wet but filled with fierce determination. "I know."

There was more he could say, but he figured they should get where they were going first. And he should get the emotions complicating this rescue mission under control.

LIZA DIDN'T TRY to keep track of the circuitous path Jamison was driving. They were getting closer to Flynn, and she was getting closer to falling apart altogether.

She should have asked one of his brothers. Or kept on trying to find Gigi herself. She never should have involved Jamison, thinking old hurts had been eradicated.

Because they weren't gone, only buried, and every

disdainful look or overly obvious statement from him dug deeper to the heart of all that old pain.

But she'd suffer through it for Gigi. She hadn't been able to save Marci from the Sons. Liza didn't know how to live having failed both her sisters. One failure was hard enough.

If she could save Gigi, get her away from the Sons, well, yeah, she wouldn't be able to go back. But going back to the Sons had only ever been to save her sisters.

Just like, once upon a time, Jamison had saved his brothers.

She could have told him. If she explained to him why she left, he would have insisted she should have told him, and *he* would have taken care of the problem.

Maybe he would have, but she'd known how hard it had been. She'd watched him put all five of his brothers before him. She'd watched him put *her* before him. To have asked him to do that again for something that was her responsibility had felt wrong.

She'd wanted to live up to the unreachable example he'd set. Instead, no matter how Liza had fought for her, Marci had thrown her life into the Sons. Liza hadn't given up on Marci, which was why she'd stayed so long, until Marci had only laughed when her boyfriend had threatened to murder Liza in her sleep if she came near them again.

By then, Carlee had been pregnant, and Liza had spent the last four years trying to talk some sense into the girl. Get them all out—she knew what it was like to be separated from your mother and she didn't want to do it to Gigi. Carlee had wavered back and forth, giving in just enough for Liza to keep hoping she could save them all.

Now Carlee was dead, Gigi was missing and the truth was Liza wasn't good enough for this. She needed the only man she knew who was.

"We'll camp here."

She sat up a little straighter, peering out the window. They'd gotten closer to the Badlands. The rock formations that made the area famous surrounded them. Craggy valleys and the eruption of rock stretched for miles, making it difficult to hide from all directions, but Liza had no doubt Jamison knew what he was doing.

"Camp?" It was still early enough spring that nights would be frigid.

"Did you think we were heading for a resort?"

She snorted. "Yeah. That's what I was expecting."

"Camper shell is set up on the bed. We'll be fine."

"Tight quarters."

"Safer that way. We'll eat a little something now. Then figure out our best bet for hideaways around Flynn."

"It's been three days since I've seen her. They could have taken her anywhere."

"Could have, but we know how they operate. Somewhere close."

"Jamison…" She didn't want to tell him. Didn't want to shift the focus away from finding Gigi, but if the whispers she heard were true, Gigi could be far, far away. "There's something more."

"Isn't there always," he muttered, pushing out of the truck.

Liza didn't know if his disgust was aimed at her or at the Sons in general, but she got out of the truck herself and crossed over to his side of the vehicle, where he was pulling out the food provisions.

"There've been rumors. Whispers. Nothing concrete and I haven't seen evidence, but if it's true..." Liza could hardly speak it. She so desperately didn't want it to be true.

Jamison put the cooler on the ground and stared expectantly at her, folding his arms over his chest when she still didn't talk. He gave her what she was sure was a very effective cop look. But she was too heartsick over Gigi to be intimidated by it.

"Trafficking," she managed to say through a too-tight throat.

"Drugs are hardly new to the Sons' operations."

"Human, Jamison. Human trafficking. Sex trafficking." She desperately tried to keep the tremor out of her voice and failed. "Gigi's such an innocent."

The impenetrable cop mask gave way to full-on horror. "She's four, you said."

"I don't know much about it, but I assume it doesn't matter how old you are. Long as a person is female and vulnerable. Hell, maybe only vulnerable. You're a cop. Surely you've seen the worst humans can do to children."

He turned away from her at that, focusing on the food.

"The point of me telling you that is if she got pulled into something…different, they're not going to follow the old rules."

He put together a sandwich and handed it to her. It took her a minute to get ahold of herself enough to take it. Despite it being her favorite—ham and Swiss, heavy on the cheese, light on the meat—she didn't have an appetite for it.

If nothing else, she could find some tiny satisfaction over the fact that he remembered what she liked to eat. That he didn't only remember the ways she'd betrayed him.

"The Sons do things a certain way," he said, making his own sandwich. "Even if it's new, the ways will be old. They evolve, but they don't change. We just have to figure out where they'd be able to hide human cargo instead of drugs. I think we can."

"You're awfully confident."

"You came to me for a reason, Liza. I have to believe it's because you thought I could do this."

Since she didn't trust her voice, she nodded.

"Then I'll do it."

Chapter Six

Jamison was pretty sure they hadn't been tailed, and they had a few hours before anyone in the Sons figured out their location. The tails would have tried to follow or figure out where he'd gone before contacting their superiors—probably not his father or Liza's. These geniuses were too low in the pecking order. So, the chain of communication would take time.

Once they sent more men—better trackers—it'd still take a good hour. Too many places to look—and he was still a distance from Flynn, which was naturally where the men would start their search.

But even knowing he had a few hours of safety, he wasn't about to sleep on the same little air mattress in the camper shell of Grandma's truck with his ex.

He had supreme willpower, but he also knew better than to test it with Liza.

Instead, he took the first shift, sleeping when he knew there would be the least chance of being caught. Though he told her to wake him up in two hours, he also set the timer on his phone because he didn't quite trust her.

He shouldn't trust her at all—with anything. This human trafficking thing could be a crock for all he knew.

But why would it be? Jamison certainly couldn't put it past the old man. Even though Liza might have lied to him once upon a time, he had a hard time believing even now that she was the kind of woman who could lie about her sister being in trouble like that.

Which probably made him an *excellent* mark.

He sighed. He could sleep with the best of them in the worst situations, but not with all this doubt and uncertainty.

Still, he wanted Liza to think he'd slept. That way she'd be more likely to sleep herself.

If this wasn't a giant con.

He pulled his phone out of his pocket. No service here, which he'd known going in. Still, he typed in a text to Cody and Brady about the potential of the Sons being involved in human trafficking. If he got into a place with service, the text would go through. Hopefully.

He put the phone back in his pocket and then pulled out the map of South Dakota. It was worn in the creases, and no doubt there were more high-tech ways to keep his records, but Jamison preferred what he could see spread out before him.

This wasn't the same map he'd shown Liza last night, which was up in the front of the truck. This was his personal map, and how he'd been keeping tabs on the Sons for most of his life. Even before he'd escaped and become an officer of the law.

He'd marked everything he'd known while he'd been in. Anyplace they hid people or drugs. Their entire array of camps over the years. Crimes. Disappearances. Deaths.

A story of all the things he hadn't been able to prevent. After Dev's near-death run-in with the Sons, Ace in particular, Jamison had given up on taking them down and had instead focused on keeping what he could and whom he could safe.

All along he'd marked this map every time he heard something, hadn't he? So, it hadn't been giving up, no matter what he told himself. Maybe he'd just been waiting for the right opportunity.

He let out a slow breath. If he was only putting himself in danger, it wouldn't worry him. But it wasn't just him. Liza was here, too.

Jamison shoved that thought away. She was in danger because she wanted to be. He couldn't let that weigh on his conscience. Besides, she'd be in a heck of a lot more hot water if he *wasn't* here.

He studied the map. Flynn was a speck. Mostly a ghost town when Jamison had been growing up, and he imagined it still was. With the addition of the Sons camp.

They wouldn't keep Gigi there, and if Liza's trafficking story was right on, they'd be very careful.

What little Jamison knew about human trafficking wasn't pretty. He had a feeling Cody would know more. Maybe he should drive until they got service, get in touch with his brother.

But that would draw attention and he wanted to lie as low as he could. Whenever Dad's men arrived, and they would arrive, it would give Jamison an indication of what they were trying to hide.

There weren't many of Jamison's marks around Flynn on the map. Flynn was sacred ground to Dad. Where he'd been born. Where his parents had left him to die. Where he, in his mind, rose from the ashes as a poor castoff to the deadliest man in South Dakota.

Flynn was Dad's mecca. If he was having the whole gang camp there in his sacred spot, something was escalating. Was it the human trafficking?

If so, the hiding area would be somewhere close, but not too close. If Jamison had to guess, it would be somewhere in the buttes and gullies. Caves, maybe. Isolated, surely. Would they bring potential buyers there, or ship the cargo off?

If they were shipping, they'd go west into Wyoming. Best chance of being undetected while moving groups of people.

There were too many possibilities after that. Denver…farther west. Jamison folded Wyoming and Colorado out of view. Focus on one thing at a time. Narrow down the options to locate where they were potentially holding Gigi.

It would be somewhere west of Flynn, but not into the national park. Too easy and possible to be accidentally stumbled upon.

Jamison planned on canvassing from the national park line out toward Flynn. He tried not to think of the huge, nearly impossible task of finding people who didn't want to be found in the great, empty landscape beyond the national park.

When he got into cell range he'd call Felicity, see if she'd heard of any strange goings-on around the park. One of the Knight girls who was now a park ranger, Felicity was too dang nice to hold a grudge against Liza. She'd probably jump right in to help.

But that would only be when and if they got into cell service range. For now... Well, he'd stop pretending he was sleeping. Liza could get a few hours and he could make all sorts of contingency plans as he waited and watched for his father's men to hunt them down.

And lead them exactly where he wanted to go.

He opened the camper shell and slid out, already scanning his surroundings.

Liza nearly jerked where she was standing, something gold and familiar in her hand. She fisted her fingers over it, then stood there, still as a statue.

"Thought you were going to sleep longer," she offered when he did nothing more than crouch at the shell's opening.

He barely heard her over the awful pounding of his heart.

"What's that?" he demanded, even though he knew exactly what it was. Even though the last thing he wanted was confirmation. Not with the past whipping around them in the wind.

She looked down at her fisted hand, then met his gaze with defiance and sadness in her own. He'd been so convinced that if he got her out of the Sons he could get rid of that misery. But he'd been eighteen and foolish.

"You know what it is," she said, and he shouldn't have been able to hear her with the way the Dakota winds were swirling with their usual violence.

But he did.

"Why do you still have it?" Which was another question he didn't actually want an answer to. But somehow the questions kept falling out of his mouth, like his brain wasn't in charge—something instinctual was.

"You told me it was good luck," she said, opening her fingers and letting the chain dangle from them. The heart locket twirled in the wind. "Figured I'd need some of that in my life—now more than ever."

Too many questions piled up in his brain. Most of all: Was the same picture still inside that stupid locket?

It didn't matter. None of the questions about the past mattered. So, he'd focus on the surroundings, on the next move. He'd concentrate on anything except the way she looked down at the locket in her fist like it held all the answers to her broken dreams.

Walking among the ghosts between them was emotional suicide. It complicated everything and, most of all, it did not matter.

But his heart couldn't seem to let it go the way his brain urged him to. "Why did you leave?"

LIZA DIDN'T MOVE. She was afraid that if she did, she'd move toward him instead of far, far away.

"I thought you had it all figured out," she said, not daring to look at him. He'd see all the pain that was surely radiating from her like the dust the wind picked up and swirled between them.

He turned away with no small amount of disgust. She still knew him well enough to know the loathing was aimed inward. He didn't want to ask her questions like that. He wanted to be above the past.

But he wasn't. Something stirred inside her that would be close to deadly here in this moment, but she'd never been very adept at knowing what was good for her.

It was so hard to watch him be the man she'd always known he'd grow into. Hard to feel all those same emotions she thought time had eradicated. Could he love a woman he hadn't seen for fifteen years? *Someone whom he hated*, she thought.

He couldn't.

Maybe the locket was good luck, though, even with all these conflicting emotions, because Jamison's gaze went to the horizon, hard and cold. It was different than even back in Bonesteel before she'd been shot. There had been a heat to his disdain then.

This was pure, deadly cold.

Which stirred something inside her, too. That old need to soothe him, to give him the warmth everything about the Sons had dimmed into that coldness.

"Get in the truck," he ordered.

She didn't argue, didn't try to see what he saw, because there was no doubt in her mind the Sons had found them.

She got in the truck.

Back then, she'd fought Jamison tooth and nail more often than not, but these days she was grateful to have someone take the lead. She was tired of trying to stay one step ahead of the Sons and failing.

Jamison slid into the driver's seat, opening a map on his lap. He took a pencil from the middle console and marked a few things.

"What are you doing?" she asked, hoping the question didn't sound like an accusation. But men were after them and he was taking notes?

"We've got three cars—I'm guessing two men apiece. They're all coming from the west. So, we'll head there. Grab that pack there in the back."

He kept looking at the map while she struggled to pull the giant, heavy backpack into the front seat.

He made a few more notes on his map, and then carefully folded it and shoved it into his pocket. He took the bag from her, nodding into the back again. "Grab the smaller one. We're going on a hike. Your leg up for it?"

Even if it wasn't, she would have nodded. She wasn't about to be the person holding Jamison back. Not when she was the reason he was here in the first place.

She snatched the pack and followed his lead getting back out of the truck. She didn't see anything on the horizon to the west, except maybe some up-turned dust. Still, she trusted Jamison's instincts.

They shouldered their individual packs. Without any verbal instruction, Liza knew to fall in step behind Jamison. Her leg hurt, but it was a low-level, throbbing ache she'd get used to.

And if she didn't, she'd just think of Gigi in danger and suck it up.

He led her down into a valley, over the crumbling rock that made up the strange formations that drew sightseers every year. They weren't as big or uninterrupted here as they were in the national park. Here there were still gaps of flat land with early green grass growing.

She tried not to make a sound when she stumbled and hit her leg the wrong way. Jamison didn't look back at her, his attention focused on what she assumed was the path in his mind.

"Why are we leaving the truck behind?" Liza asked as she skidded on a rock and just barely stopped herself from stumbling over a dangerous edge.

"We're going to hike around, let them think we abandoned the vehicle. They'll start looking for us on foot, and they'll probably start from the truck and move toward the target. If we circle up and around, we can get back to the truck in a few hours. From the direction they came, I've got a few ideas about where a trafficking hideout might be."

"What if they guard the truck? Or torch it?"

She could tell he hadn't thought of that, because

his forward motion paused almost imperceptibly. "They won't torch it. Their prime objective is to find us, and likely bring us in front of our fathers. The truck is inconsequential."

Liza didn't bother to argue as she looked back at the truck, a sitting duck for the destruction the Sons liked to inflict on anything in their path.

Jamison no doubt had it right that if they were caught they'd be brought in front of their fathers and the "council." Judgment would be meted out, and Liza shuddered to think what awful things might be waiting for her and Jamison.

But she didn't think his assessment of what could happen with the truck was right—at all.

Chapter Seven

They hiked for a good hour. He had the route fixed in his mind, but still, he used his compass to make sure they weren't getting turned around in the rock formations that could start to look all the same if one didn't know how to navigate them.

The sun slowly started its descent, and Jamison began to lead them back to the truck. He was pretty sure he'd timed it right, but he still kept the pace slow and steady—Liza behind him rather than next to him—as they got closer and closer to where he'd left the truck.

He wanted to be back there by the time the sun went down. It would get exponentially colder as the day wore on, and while he'd packed Liza some warmer gear, he doubted she needed a long hike in the cold with her current injuries.

She'd held up like a champ and he opened his mouth to tell her so but closed it instead. She didn't need his encouragement. She was trying to save her sister. Not earn brownie points with him.

He wasn't her protector anymore, even if she'd

come and asked him for a hand. Help wasn't the same as saving someone. He didn't need to rescue her. Just like all of these feelings wrapping around him would go away. It was memory, not reality.

They meant nothing to each other. Nothing at all.

He'd get it through his thick skull eventually.

There was a tinge to the air as they approached the truck, and a low-level dread crept across his skin. The acrid smell of fire and chemicals became more and more potent the closer they got to the vehicle.

Still, he wouldn't let himself believe the worst. What possible reason would they have had to burn the truck? It would draw notice—and the one thing the Sons had always shied away from was too much attention from the law.

But as he closed in on the clearing, he could see the dark smoke. They stepped level with the truck and all Jamison could do was stop and stare.

They'd torched it, just as Liza had worried about. It smoked, the blackened wreckage of his grandmother's truck a grotesque twisted skeletal remain on the dusty landscape. An incongruous image against the riotous sunset.

Jamison tried not to let it get to him, but it was living proof he'd gone soft. He'd been sure they wouldn't bother, so certain he knew what they were planning and how to defeat them. His stomach twisted and pitched at all the ways he'd been wrong—and all he might still miscalculate before this fool's mission was over.

"Grandma Pauline is going to kick your butt,"

Liza said with some amusement. The sunset was a splash of brilliant colors behind her. A sure sign a storm would roll in halfway through the night.

All they had were the packs on their back.

Kick his butt? Grandma was going to skin him. *If* they made it out of this alive. For the first time he fully understood why Liza had been so scared, why she'd come to him as a last resort. Lives were on the line—in a way they hadn't been as much when they'd been kids—or at least in a way he hadn't fully grasped when he'd been a teenager full of self-righteous outrage.

Worst of all, Liza didn't seem any kind of surprised. She'd warned him, hadn't she? He could only stare at the wreckage and wonder…

He'd saved his five brothers, and Liza for as long as she'd let that last. The Wyatt boys had built lives of their own, and while they hadn't brought down the Sons, they'd survived them. Escaped them. It was supposed to be enough. After Dev's close call, Jamison had told himself it was.

It burned like acid in his gut that he'd done exactly what Liza had told him not to do: underestimate the Sons. All because once upon a time he'd considered escape a win.

It had taken all of his thirty-seven years, but he finally accepted wholly and fully that escape and survival weren't a win. Not fully. Not yet.

"They're not the Sons you used to know, Jamison," Liza said softly. As if she was comforting him instead of saying "I told you so."

He'd kept tabs, though. He'd watched. How could he not have seen they were different now? Bolder. Surer. Far more dangerous.

"You have to know what unchecked power does to men," Liza continued, as if every emotion and thought was broadcast across his face. Which it might be. Which was as unacceptable as this miscalculation.

"It grows and grows until there is nothing left. No one challenges them. Everyone fears them. Even the bigger agencies haven't bothered trying to infiltrate in years. The Sons have everything they ever wanted, but they will always want more. So, they will destroy and destroy and destroy. Because nothing can stop them."

She'd started out unmoved. Resigned, almost, but as she spoke the emotion crept into her voice and vibrated there. And deep inside him.

"They were bad enough then," he said, still not able to wrap his mind around her words. How could they be stronger, more feared? How was it possible? Right was supposed to win—he'd won all those years ago.

Except right hadn't won. It had just escaped.

"They're worse now," Liza said with a conviction he no longer questioned.

Facts were facts, and the fact was that the Sons he'd known wouldn't have bothered. They wouldn't have wanted to draw attention with a burned-out truck in the middle of nowhere.

If what Liza said was true, and they'd grown and

the powers that be had stopped their periodic attempts to infiltrate and disband…

He blew out a breath, letting concern out with it. Because he needed a new plan, and emotion wouldn't get him anywhere. Not guilt or failure or weakness.

He glanced at Liza, who was watching the smoke as if it were just an average sight. Care wouldn't get him anywhere, either, but it sat there in his gut like an old illness he hadn't fully cured.

But remembering that time, and the boy he'd been, Jamison realized he needed to access that person again. Find his youthful certainty. His adolescent arrogance. He had to be ready to risk anything again.

The goal wouldn't be *escape* this time. There would be an end.

He'd been resigned to the fact that getting involved *might* bring him into contact with his father again, *might* be the tipping point for his father's eventual revenge.

But now he understood there was no *might* about it. It was time to end what he'd let fester and grow and rot the landscape he loved so much.

He stared at the truck and gave up everything he'd chosen to bury in the past fifteen years. He let it go on the wind. Maybe he'd subconsciously known this was coming, because there was only a little pain, quickly smothered by the cold certainty that had made up his teenage years.

"Unchecked power gets checked eventually, Liza. No one gets to rule forever."

"And when would that eventually come to pass?"

she asked, as if she didn't see the change in him. As if she couldn't feel the change in the air.

He looked back at her then, met her furious and frightened, dark gaze, orange and red blazing behind her like the apocalypse was already coming for them.

It was. It was time.

They'd find Gigi.

Then he'd go after the Sons.

"It gets checked now."

THE LOOK ON Jamison's face made her shiver for more than one reason. It reminded her of the boy she'd known.

And loved.

Which was a terrible thing to be thrust into—those old feelings, made more potent by the fact they *weren't* teenagers anymore. This wasn't about *freedom* anymore.

It was about her sister's life, and maybe theirs.

The tremor was fear, but it was also something deeper, something more elemental. A sensation she would not under any circumstances let herself acknowledge.

She sincerely hoped.

"What are we going to do?" she asked, her voice barely more than a whisper.

He frowned, considered the landscape, then pinned her with another too-potent stare. "What do you think we should do?"

"What?"

"You were right about the truck. You…" He shook

his head almost imperceptibly. "I thought I'd been keeping tabs, but clearly not well enough. You know them, have a better understanding of their moves than I do."

"I'm not *one* of them, Jamison. When will you—"

"I didn't say you were. I said you know them. We need to use that understanding, because I can't anticipate their moves anymore."

"I don't—"

"You'll stop that now."

She was too shocked by the snap in his tone to give him a piece of her mind.

"You know. You've been living inside the Sons for fifteen years. You don't have to pretend I know more than you. I'm not going to punish you for it."

"That isn't what I—"

He merely raised an eyebrow and she trailed off. He was right, partially. She was too used to the habit of pretending she didn't know anything—to save her skin. She was used to using all her skills and knowledge on the sly.

She wasn't used to…a partner. She didn't want one. "I'm tired, Jamison," she said, trying to keep her voice from breaking. "I've been fighting this battle for too long. You know what that feels like."

"Yeah. And I know you can't quit until Gigi is safe. But you have me, Liza. I'm not asking you to do this on your own. I'm asking you to use your brain."

"You always did it on your own."

"No, I didn't. My brothers and you were all old enough to hold your own when I helped you escape.

Gigi is four. Besides, you said it yourself. They're more dangerous now. So, we need to work together. If you were alone—what would you do next?"

Liza scrubbed her hands over her face. Her leg ached, and so did her head. Her eyes were gritty from the dust in the wind and she desperately wanted to go to sleep.

But if she was alone, she'd press on. To somewhere she thought Gigi might be. "I'd just keep looking. They won't have given up on trying to find us. Burning the truck was a message. But you were right earlier—it isn't our fathers out searching for us, so they're not going to kill us. But they want to find us—bringing us to our fathers? Jackpot."

"Why didn't your father do anything to you when you went back?"

Liza didn't react to that question. It was one of the ones she'd been ready for. Still, the glib lie or clever redirect didn't flow off her tongue like she'd practiced.

"Just another thing I'm underestimating, isn't it?"

His voice was far too soft, far too much like the boy she remembered. "Women don't mean as much there. You know that." She kept her back to him and closed her eyes against how pathetic that lie sounded.

"Loyalty matters. Above all else."

"Yeah, well. I survived, didn't I? The task at hand is getting to Gigi. They'll know that she's what I'm after. If they're smart, they'll just lie in wait."

"If?"

"It's not that they're not smart, but they're cocky.

Some can be impatient with Ace's orders, trying to move up the chain. I've noticed…" She trailed off but Jamison only waited. It was hard to break the habit of keeping her thoughts, her theories to herself. But he was right. They had to do this together—not him or her, but them. "Ace's best men? I haven't seen them around much. It's just a hunch, but I thought maybe they were put in charge of the trafficking. Which would leave his next tier with the job of finding us. They're not the top tier for a reason, though."

"More brawn than brains?"

She nodded. Some things he still understood.

"Hence the torched truck. All right. So, we'll keep heading toward Flynn. Do you think they'll come back?"

Liza looked around. Daylight was fading. In the east, darkness was beginning to twinkle with the first hint of stars. She could feel the temperature dropping already and the wind gave no sign of letting up.

"Not tonight. They'll spend the night closer to the other men. They'll check in with either our fathers or whoever their direct orders are coming from. They'll revise their plan and move out at daybreak."

"And whoever is in charge of the trafficking will likely be getting ready to mobilize. They won't wait."

"I don't know if it's true," Liza said, and this time not because she was afraid of voicing her opinion. But because she desperately didn't want it to be true. She had to believe it was *possible* she was over-reacting.

But when she met Jamison's gaze it was too… kind. And laced with pity. She turned away. "We need to move through the night, get a head start on them if we can."

"Agreed." He moved over to her, but she didn't dare look up. She felt him unzip her pack and then slide it off her shoulders. When she finally worked up the nerve to look at him, he was holding out a sweatshirt. "Put this on, then the coat. Lose the leather."

She wanted to argue, but she had *some* common sense. The sweatshirt and the coat he held in his hand would keep her far warmer than her thin coat ever would. Still, the old leather coat was something of a talisman. It had survived and so had she.

He sighed, and as if reading her mind, shook out the sweatshirt, then did the honors himself. He pulled the sweatshirt over her head—and over the jacket. Then he held out the coat.

Swallowing against the lump in her throat, she slid one arm in, and then the other. Before she could move to zip it up herself, he did it.

Too close. Too Jamison. She wanted to lean forward because she knew, no matter how many reservations he still had about her, no matter how much bitterness he still held on to over the way she'd left, he'd hold her and tell her it would be okay.

Which would break her completely. So, she stood statue-still as he zipped up the coat.

"I've done this before," he said, that quiet sureness she remembered about him threading through those words. Making her waver against the determination not to lean into him. "I can do it again."

She let that break the spell. She'd once thought him infallible magic, but she didn't believe anyone was that anymore. "Don't make promises you don't know you can keep, Jamison. You'll only beat yourself up about it later."

"I'll beat myself up about it either way," he muttered, releasing the zipper. "If you need a break, a rest, a snack, speak up. Best we keep our strength up."

He hefted the pack onto her back again, then pulled two headlamps out of his. He handed her one. "Put it on your head, but leave the light off and stay close to me for as much of the hike as you can." He pulled the small light onto his head, illuminating the space between them.

Then he handed her a gun.

Chapter Eight

Once Jamison made a decision, he didn't waver. Usually. But handing a woman he didn't fully trust a loaded gun while ordering her to hike behind him left him vulnerable.

Hell, if he was going to go now, it might as well be at Liza's hand behind his back. Symbolic, and surely the rightful end to his own stupidity.

But as they set off, his own loaded gun strapped to his side, Liza didn't make any moves to turn the weapon on him. She kept her headlamp on her head, but the light off. Which meant she walked close enough to him that his light guided them both.

He couldn't watch her for signs of her limp worsening or her expression for signs of fatigue, but after at least a good hour of harrowing hiking in the dark, he decided to take it upon himself to say they needed a break.

He handed her a bottle of water and a protein bar and considered himself something of a saint for not lecturing her when she grimaced at it and stuck it in her coat pocket rather than eat it.

"We should change your bandage."

She shook her head. "Not yet. We need to be closer. Besides, it feels fine."

He doubted it very much, but studying her in the eerie glow of his lamplight didn't show any undue signs of pain or worry. It would take up too much valuable time to argue with her, so he nodded, took another swig of water and then packed it all away.

They started out again. He kept on the lookout for signs of human and animal life. Bobcats were a concern, as was stumbling upon a sleeping anything. Then there were the rattlers—dangerous this time of year if only because disturbing rock as they hiked might accidentally unearth a den.

The last thing either of them needed was a run-in with the kind of wildlife that could injure them. Especially in the dark, without cell service and with a biker gang looking for them.

So, Jamison kept a slow, careful pace—refusing to let the irritation or impatience gain purchase. Maybe they were racing against the clock, but he doubted the Sons were racing against the same one. And if they were, he'd have to deal with that, but not at the expense of making a mistake here and now.

For now, slow and steady was the best they could do, and he could not let the driving need to get closer, faster, push him into doing something dumb.

He kept watch of the time, making sure they stopped and had a snack or drink each hour. Each time, he checked her over.

On the third stop, knowing they were getting

closer to Flynn and they'd have to be even more careful so as not to stumble across members of the Sons, he looked her over with a critical eye.

She appeared tired, but he was sure he did, too. She'd stopped walking, so he couldn't assess her limp, but as he looked down at where the wound was, he swore. There was blood seeping into the pants Grandma had given her this morning—which meant she had probably broken a stitch and was bleeding through her bandage. "We need to change the dressing on your leg."

"We don't have time."

"I'll be quick."

"Trying to get me naked again. It's tiresome."

"As tiresome as that joke." He dropped his pack, pulled out the first aid kit. "You must have busted a stitch. You need a tighter bandage. If that doesn't stop bleeding…"

"Yeah, yeah, yeah," she muttered. She pushed the pants down past the bandage that was completely soaked with blood.

"This isn't good."

"It could be a heck of a lot worse."

True enough, and they didn't have time to argue over it. He removed the bloody gauze and packed it up in one of the zipper bags he'd brought. He did his best to disinfect in the cold, dusty wind and the dim light of his headlamp.

She shivered in the cold, and he worked as fast and efficiently as he could. It looked like only one stitch had broken, so he did his best to tighten the bandage over it. She needed to be in a hospital. If this got worse, she'd be more liability than help.

He opened his mouth to say just that, but then thought better of it. Liza was the one dealing with the pain. She wanted to save her sister. She knew what she was doing. It wasn't his job to police her.

It never had been, and he frowned at the thought he might have done it anyway. Had he been the reason she left? He'd been too heavy-handed in trying to keep her safe and she'd escaped to the only place she'd known to go?

Senseless questions. Useless thoughts. It did not matter, and he had to stop letting his mind go to the past.

But as he stood after patching her up and putting away the first aid kit, he had to accept that whether or not he wanted to deal with the past, it was here. Always in the air between them, an electricity that seemed to charge off each other. It was the past, it was attraction and it was as potent as it had been back then.

There was too much still *here*—maybe it was the unfinished ending they'd had or maybe it was something deeper—but it seemed to thicken and get harder to fight against.

They stood too close, looked at each other too long, and no matter that he knew his brain was cautioning him to move, to focus, to *stop*, he hovered exactly where he was. Too close to her. Too tempted to…

"You'd only hate yourself as much as you hate

me," Liza whispered, breaking that moment. Thank God.

He would hate himself, she had that right, but something about the pitch-black night made it easier to access the full, awful truth, instead of burying it down deep. "Being hurt and hate aren't the same thing, Liza. Don't conflate that. They do. I won't."

He stepped back, letting her fix her pants over the bandage herself.

"It must be nice to have just left the Sons, cut out all that horror and be perfect and happy now," she said, her voice harsh and full of emotion here in the dark. "It must be so nice to have left it all behind."

"You could have," he reminded her, though it didn't come out harsh. He was starting to feel a tiredness creep in, which drained him of the energy to maintain a facade of strength. It left only the truth.

"No, I couldn't."

"If you say so."

"Marci was still in there."

He didn't want to get into the whys of her leaving. Or perhaps more honestly, he desperately wanted to get into it and knew it wouldn't satisfy either of them. "Your sister didn't want to be saved. It's why we left her in the first place. You said you were fine with it. I don't know why the four years you were out would have changed that."

"That's it for you? You don't try to save someone you love just because they don't want to be saved?"

He noted she didn't address all the holes he'd just punched in her argument, but he didn't need to keep falling into potholes of the past. He needed to complete this mission and move on before that temptation took him someplace he didn't want to be. "Not if you plan on saving yourself."

"You couldn't understand. You didn't have to leave anyone behind."

It was painful that she could think that. That anything he'd done then or now had been *easy*. That there was anything *nice* about knowing your father was a monster and if you weren't careful that perversion might bloom inside you, too.

So, instead of responding, he walked on.

HER LEG HURT so much she wanted to cry. Her heart hurt just as much. At too many things. Not just the way he'd gently rebandaged her wound, or the way he'd looked at her afterward—like no time had passed at all. But at what he'd said, at the way he'd dismissed Marci, and at the shock of hurt on his face when she'd said he'd left nothing behind.

Then he'd blanked it all away and started walking again.

Remorse pulsed inside her like a heartbeat. Regret twined around her lungs, making it hard to breathe without crying.

But she forged ahead because Gigi was what was important, not her screwed-up past or any lingering feelings she had for Jamison Wyatt.

Being hurt and hate aren't the same thing, Liza. Don't conflate that.

Those words would haunt her until the day she

died. Because all she'd ever known growing up was hate and hurt. She hadn't seen a sparkle of goodness anywhere except in the Wyatt boys, and then out there in the world Jamison had given her.

Maybe there were more reasons she hadn't been able to stay out there than just Marci. Maybe all that goodness of Grandma Pauline and the Knights had been too much to bear. Too good to accept when all she'd ever known was bad.

What a horribly depressing thought. But she had to cut herself *some* slack. She'd been twenty. Maybe things would have been different if she'd been younger, or older.

But things couldn't be different, because she'd made her choices. Just like Marci had made hers. Carlee hers.

But Gigi didn't have choices.

So, Liza kept moving, ignoring the pain in her leg. But she couldn't quite ignore the pain in her heart, too. "Did you ever want to go back?"

If he was surprised by the question, he didn't act it. "I don't know."

She'd expected an emphatic no, or a certainty at the very least, not *I don't know*. That was enough to throw her already unbalanced world even more off-kilter. Jamison *always* knew.

"What do you mean you don't know?" she demanded.

"It's too complicated," he replied, moving forward at a quicker pace that had her scurrying to catch up with him.

"That's not an answer, Jamison."

He sighed heavily. "The answer lies somewhere in the middle. It was home, much as I hated it. He's my father, much as I hate him. I didn't want to *go back*, but there were days I didn't...*not* want to go back."

She shook her head, as if she could negate what was clearly an honest answer. She knew that churn too well, wanting both things in the same breath. Never being quite right.

And she'd never been able to express that to anyone, but Jamison had distilled it into a few words. Ones that would probably only ever make sense to them.

Now was hardly the time to wade into it, but if not now—when? When would she ever be able to talk about this with someone? Jamison was the only one who understood both sides of the life. "If it was complicated to stay away, don't you think it was complicated to go back?"

Jamison was quiet for a while, but eventually he responded, though he sidestepped the question. "Conflicted or not. I didn't go back. That's the difference."

"I *had* to go back."

"If that's what you need to tell yourself, Liza, go ahead. You don't need me to absolve you of your choices. If you needed that, you wouldn't have left."

She stopped walking at that, because it was true. She didn't need his approval or his forgiveness. If she'd asked herself a day ago, she would have said she didn't want it.

But here in the middle of the howling, frigid dark, her leg pulsing with pain and her heart aching, she realized that was what she'd been craving since she'd sneaked out of the Knights' house all those years ago.

His approval. His forgiveness.

She was too old for both. Too old for this.

"As far as I'm concerned, it doesn't matter," Jamison said, still moving, far enough away she had to flip on her own lamp to catch up without tripping. "We're here for one thing and one thing only."

"Gigi."

Which meant she had to give all that acceptance and forgiveness to herself, rather than waiting for Jamison to give it to her.

She blew out a breath. It was a shaking realization, and yet it took no weight off her shoulders. Not until Gigi was safe. Once Gigi was safe, Liza could build her own life.

Her *own* life. Anywhere and anyhow she pleased. Regardless of Jamison or the Sons.

She breathed again, letting her heart beat in time with the pulse of her wounds. She'd use all that *hurt* to drive her through the fear. Straight into a future no one but her got to dictate.

She caught up to Jamison, flicking off her light once she was close enough to walk in the beam of his. They walked in silence, which Liza figured was for the best.

No more talking. No more trying to get him to believe or see something in her. It didn't matter. She just had to *remember* that. Remember *those* words of not needing his absolution over the words of hurt and hate.

They didn't hate each other. They didn't have to forgive each other.

They just had to forgive themselves. She wondered if he ever had, and doubted it very, very much.

Jamison stopped abruptly, quickly turning off his headlamp. Liza sucked in a breath and held it. Far off in the distance, something flickered. Firelight, if she had to guess.

Chapter Nine

"That'll be a camp of some kind. All of them?" Jamison glanced back at Liza because he was determined to rely on her information as much as his own instincts.

She had an odd expression on her face. The fear and uncertainty were gone. Even the snarky, careless mask she'd worn at first was missing.

She looked fierce. Determined. He glanced at her leg—as far as he could tell, the bandage was holding and no new blood was leaking out.

"Probably all of the ones looking for us. Most of them at the very least," she said with complete certainty.

"You stay here and—"

"No. Never separate," Liza said emphatically, which might have swayed him if those words and the way she said them didn't remind him of his father.

"That's a Sons rule."

"It's a smart one," she said, not wavering. "If we're going to outwit them, we need to play by their rules."

"Never."

"Jamison, I won't let your pride or honor or baggage or whatever you want to call it get in the way here. You said you were ready to check their power and face them and your father. You know you can't do it as a cop. You have to do it as Jamison Wyatt."

I'd rather die. He didn't say it out loud because he knew how words like *die* could become a little too real when dealing with the Sons. "I won't be Ace, Liza. I can't be."

"I'm not saying you have to be, Jamison. But we have to fight with some of the ruthlessness they do or we'll never survive."

Ruthlessness. He hated that word. As a cop he'd had to harden himself to things. Injustices he'd dreamed of solving. As he'd told Liza, some people didn't want to be saved—and you couldn't survive yourself if you were always trying to save them anyway. But ruthlessness was more than that. It was a loss of humanity—a blackness on your soul.

He'd watched that blackness swallow his father more and more with every year. Because unlike most of his brothers, he could still remember flashes of a man who wasn't *all* bad. At one point, there'd been *some* compassion in Ace Wyatt.

Jamison had never known what exactly eradicated it bit by bit, but he knew it was a slippery slope. The more hurt you inflicted, the less goodness you had inside you—and it didn't always matter if the people you were hurting deserved it.

Slippery slope or not, there was a little four-year-old girl in far more danger than he'd ever been. So,

Liza had one thing right. He couldn't play by the cop rules he was used to. He couldn't toe the line of the law like he wanted to.

Ruthless, no, he couldn't promise that. But he'd come here for a reason, and she was right enough that if he was going to check the power of his Sons, and face his father once and for all, he had to be willing to cross some lines he'd promised himself he wouldn't.

But not all of them.

"I can't promise to be ruthless, Liza. I've made too many promises to myself about not becoming Ace. But for a little girl caught up in something that isn't right or fair, I'll do whatever it takes."

She let out a breath, but before she could talk anymore, he forged forward.

"We need to know how many men they have. I think it'd be better, safer and smarter if only one of us got close enough to count. I think since I'm the one without a gunshot wound, it would make the most sense if it was me."

"And if they find you, take you to your father, where does that leave me?"

"The more we know—"

"No. That's the cop talking. We don't need to know what they're doing. We need to know what *we're* doing. We're after Gigi, not them. So, we avoid. What if we hiked around them, keep heading toward Flynn? Surely wherever they're holding Gigi is somewhere between them and Flynn."

"Beyond Flynn. West. It makes it easier to either

transport or have a meeting place without bringing outsiders into town," Jamison muttered, vaguely irritated her plan was better.

"So, we hike beyond. Avoid as much detection as possible."

She had a point. He doubted Dad's scouts expected them to hike through the night. If they could get past this group before the sun rose, then they'd only have to worry about camp lookouts, presumably.

If they could get around Flynn before sunrise? Their chances were even better.

"Get out that map of yours. The one with the marks," she ordered.

He shifted his pack and pulled the map out of his pocket. "No headlamps. Hold this while I get my penlight out."

He handed her the map, shrugged off his pack and sifted around until his fingers brushed the slim plastic of his small, precise flashlight.

"Hold out the map," he instructed.

She did, and he studied it with the light, but as they stood there in silence, he stiffened.

A rustle. It could be animal—most likely was, but the hairs on the back of Jamison's neck stood on end. He met Liza's shadowy gaze in the dim penlight. She opened her mouth, but he quickly reached forward and placed his palm over it.

He switched off the light in his other hand and shoved it into his pocket. He needed Liza to fold the map and put it away without him actually saying the words. With his free hand, he reached out until he found one of her hands still gripping the map.

She nodded imperceptibly against the hand on her mouth, so he let his arm drop. Then he took both her hands and pulled them together—trying to get it across that he wanted her to fold up the map. It took a few seconds, but then she finally seemed to get the message.

He turned toward the noise, shielding her body with his. The folding of the map made the hint of a *swish* against the quiet, pulsing dark, but just like the rustle he'd heard—someone could mistake it for animal or the wind.

His hand itched to reach for his gun, but a shot would echo through the canyons and quiet night and give them away. He could fight off one or two, but he doubted they'd survive a whole group of the Sons descending on them.

There was nothing around him but a thick blackness his eyes hadn't adjusted to after looking at the map with the penlight. He listened through the off-and-on wind for a sound that might give him an idea of which direction the prowler was coming from. Luckily, Liza was behind him, pressed to a rock, so they couldn't be surrounded on all sides.

Unless someone came over the top of the rock outcropping.

He heard a *swish*—a knife being unsheathed, if he had to guess. Jamison had his own knife, but he kept it in his boot. The blade was short as well, and wouldn't be useful if he had to use it to defend himself in the dark.

Liza's hand pressed into the small of his back, and the other one curled around his right arm and pulled it back. She unclenched his fist and pressed something to his palm.

The handle of a knife. He couldn't see it, but based on the weight it had a longer blade than the one in his boot. He couldn't lunge blindly—it was too risky. He needed to see his target and act with as little noise as possible.

The Sons usually did this kind of thing with radios or walkies. If there was a man out there, he'd turned his off. Which gave Jamison some hope they could neutralize this threat without detection—at least for a little while.

But he needed light. And a whole hell of a lot of luck.

So, Liza's knife in hand and ready to move, he switched on his headlamp and saw just what he'd hoped he wouldn't. A man not ten feet away from them—luckily blinded by the sudden light.

Jamison lunged, hoping the element of surprise did everything he'd need it to, to keep himself and Liza safe.

LIZA SWALLOWED THE scream that welled up inside her at the last minute. Noise would likely mean capture.

Jamison's headlamp flew off his head as he jumped for the man who'd been lurking around them. The light bounced against the rock below, creating enough of a beam that Liza could make out two figures grappling in the dark.

But not who was who. Too many times, the light flashed against something bright and silver. If Liza wasn't mistaken, both men had knives as they rolled and grunted.

She couldn't try to shoot—and not just because she might hit Jamison. Noise was the enemy here. They could fight off one man—

Wait. Sons never sent just one man. Liza switched on her own lamp. She looked around, but there was no one besides Jamison and the other man grunting and fighting.

She was standing next to an outcropping of rock and some pebbles tumbled down. She looked up just in time to dart out of the way as a man jumped down. She whirled to face him, half wishing she hadn't given Jamison her knife since a gun would draw too much attention.

Since she recognized the man as one of her father's lackeys, she sneered at him. "Hello, Claybourne."

"Hello, dead meat." He held a gun, but she had one thing going for her. Her father wouldn't allow his men to use it on her.

No, if she was going to be killed, it would be by her father's hand. So, she smiled. "In your dreams, sweetheart."

"You think who your daddy is protects you. There are lines even you can't cross, little girl."

She kept her smile firmly in place even as dread

pooled in her gut. She didn't believe every idle threat one of her father's personal men threw her way, but there was enough going on for her to wonder.

They had to know she was after Gigi, and if Gigi was part of the alleged human trafficking ring, would that mean anyone had leave to kill her? Was the trafficking a big enough deal that her father wouldn't care if someone besides him killed her?

It didn't matter. Not yet. Because she'd yet to interfere with anything, and no one knew she'd heard the trafficking rumors except Jamison. Jamison, who she didn't dare look at—because if he was winning against the other guy, it was best not to draw Claybourne's attention to it.

Instead, she focused on the man her father considered his best tracker, but not one of his smartest men. "And just what line am I crossing right now?" she asked with a saccharine sweetness that would make anyone's teeth hurt.

"I'd say involving the Wyatts was the first one."

"You can't kill me for that one, Claybourne. I know it and you know it."

He smiled in the beam of her headlamp. "There's a lot of room between where we are right now, and you being a dead body at my feet, isn't there?"

The sounds of the fight had stopped, and Liza knew she had to keep talking, had to keep Claybourne's attention on her. If Jamison had won, he could surprise-attack Claybourne. If the other guy had won, well, Liza was screwed either way. She couldn't fight off two men *and* cart a hurt Jamison off somewhere safe.

God, he had to be safe.

"Don't get yourself too excited. I'll go with you willingly."

Claybourne snorted. "Sure you will." He pointed the gun at her leg. "Didn't take too good care of that, did you?"

"So, you were the bad shot back in Bonesteel."

He sneered at the insult. "I shot and hit exactly where I intended."

And so will I.

Peripherally, she saw Jamison edge just barely into the beam of light. He was a few feet behind Claybourne and completely out of sight as long as Claybourne kept his gaze on her.

Jamison edged in and out of the light and she noted his mouth was bloody and he looked angrier than a taunted mountain lion. She didn't see the other man, but she didn't dare take her main gaze away from Claybourne.

If they acted together, they could maybe bring down Claybourne without making too much noise. He wouldn't want to shoot and hurt them—though he might shoot just to make enough noise to be detected.

Liza moved her gaze to the gun he held, then back to Jamison standing in the very corner of where her beam of light reached. She ignored the sharp stab of pain at the stamp of injuries already blooming across his face.

She moved her gaze to the gun and back to

Jamison again, hoping he understood her signal. And Claybourne didn't.

"What? You think you can fight me for it, little girl?" Claybourne laughed and both she and Jamison took that as the signal to move. Liza kicked out for the gun and Jamison wrapped something around Claybourne's face.

The gun clattered to the ground and whatever piece of cloth Jamison had on Claybourne muffled his screams.

Liza lunged for the gun, fumbling with it a little bit as she picked it up. She scanned the area, saw the other man tied up with rope Jamison must have gotten out of his pack. He was gagged and completely still. Dead or not, Liza wasn't sure, but it didn't matter.

"Light, Liza," Jamison ordered through clenched teeth.

Liza immediately whipped her head back so the headlamp shone over Jamison and a struggling Claybourne.

His fighting back was growing weaker as Jamison's arm held around his neck and choked him.

"I could shoot him," Liza said, noting the way blood was dripping from Jamison's mouth and his temple.

"And we'd have how many men on our tail immediately?" Jamison returned, his breathing labored as he wrestled Claybourne to the ground. "They'll be on us soon enough. You should have some rope in your pack. Get it out."

Liza did as she was told, and only when she handed it to Jamison did he release his grip from Claybourne's neck. The man gasped and wriggled, but Jamison kept him in place and quickly hogtied him just as he had the other man.

Jamison got to his feet, ripped a strip off his already torn sweatshirt and used it to create a gag.

"You're hurt," Liza said lamely as he turned to her.

"We'll deal with that later," he returned, striding quickly to where his pack was lying half-strewed-out by the other man. Quickly and carelessly he shoved the spilled contents back into his pack and shouldered it—as if he wasn't bleeding all over. He nodded toward where Claybourne had jumped from. "We move. Now."

She gave one last look at the men lying and groaning on the rocky ground—then over to where the firelight flickered. She could see shadows, but nothing concrete. Still, when these two didn't return or respond to the walkie within a certain period of time they'd come looking.

And they'd know just what happened.

So, she moved, just as Jamison instructed.

Chapter Ten

"You're still bleeding, Jamison."

He was, and his face hurt like hell, thanks to that pissant minion and his penchant for grabbing rocks and smashing them into Jamison's face. But there was only so much nightfall left.

"It'll keep."

"Yes, I hear that's what all doctors say about head injuries. They'll 'keep,' especially if you're hiking through the dark without any light or bandages."

"What do you suggest, Liza? Sit around and rest while you bandage me up as the Sons realize we took out two of their scouts?" He eyed the eastern horizon. There was a faint glow there. Dawn. He sighed. They didn't have much time. "We need to find a cave."

"A cave?"

Since he knew very well Liza was, or had been, somewhat claustrophobic and no fan of wildlife, he knew why she was questioning him. But that didn't change their reality. "They're going to be looking for us come daylight."

"Caves are full of bats and mountain lions and

bears and *snakes*." She made a disgusted noise. "I am not finding a cave."

"Well, I am," he replied, the pulsing pain in his face making him far too irritable to be kind, and threatening to make him far too irritable to think calmly and rationally.

"This wasn't the plan," Liza muttered, trudging behind him. She'd fallen more than once as they'd attempted to hike in the dark without their lamps. Everything was working against them—but he reminded himself they hadn't been captured by the Sons' scouts, so it wasn't the worst that could happen.

"No. It wasn't the plan. But plans change."

"You're alarmingly calm about all this. They could be following us. You're hurt. I'm hurt. They know for a fact we're out here and probably where we're going. And you're just… *Plans change*."

"What would you prefer? Some yelling? A rending of garments? A tantrum?"

"Actually I would *love* to see a Jamison Wyatt mantrum. Would make my entire life, I'm almost sure."

"Ha ha." He stumbled a bit on a dip in the ground, swore. He'd just about kill for a break. A nap. And yes, to clean up his bloody and hopefully not broken face. "If either of us are going to get any rest, we need a cave."

"So, we're going to crawl into a cave, risk mountain lion attack, and what?"

"Take turns sleeping during the day when it's

harder to avoid people seeing us. Eat. Clean me up. Look at the map. Let them scour the whole damn place for us. They aren't going to find us. If we find a deep enough cave. Then we move again at night. Even if they figure out what we're doing, it won't be until it's too late to find us today." He hoped.

"I hate that that's a good idea," she muttered. "How are we going to find a cave without our lights?"

"If we're in the area I think we're in, we just have to keep moving due west."

"You know where we are?"

"Hopefully." He didn't know if being familiar with this area was lucky or a terrible omen of things to come, but these canyons and caves outside Flynn had been his childhood playground—and hell—all wrapped up into one.

Dad had considered the age of seven to be a great turning point for a boy, and each passing year more of one. Every summer he'd be left for as many days as years he had been on this earth to toughen him up. Learn to be a man.

The first summer had been sheer terror and torture, but he'd lasted seven days and earned his father's praise. There had been something *magical* in watching Ace Wyatt find pride in him.

Five years later, when his father had done the same thing to Dev, everything had changed for Jamison.

He'd known then and there he had to get them out. He'd spent the rest of his childhood doing just that—and surviving every one of his father's punishments or beatings when one of his brothers disappeared.

Ace had never given Jamison enough credit to think he orchestrated the escapes, but he'd blamed Jamison's lack of courage, strength and attention to detail for them happening. Jamison had always gotten a perverse thrill out of the fact that it was Ace's lack of attention to detail when it came to his sons that had made each escape possible.

By the time Jamison had gotten Dev out—the last one—the beating from his father had almost killed him. He knew his father had considered it in that moment.

Jamison had been resigned to that. He'd saved his brothers, and he could die knowing he'd done all he could. He'd felt a little bad about his friend Liza, but such was life.

Instead, Ace had pulled back. There'd been something terrible in his gaze in that moment, but he hadn't explained it. He'd only smiled and left Jamison alone in that cave to deal with his injuries and find his way back to camp.

Here he was, nearly twenty years later, in slightly better shape—and a man with a gun—looking for that same cave. It all felt a little too circular, but it was the only thing to do.

So, he kept moving to where he thought the caves from his youth should be. Walking and ignoring all the pain in his body until he saw the first signs of large rock faces they could climb in order to find the caves.

"We'll try to go by penlight first. I'm going to

look for the cave. You're going to watch and listen for anyone else."

He worked in silence, trusting Liza to keep an eye and ear out for anything that might be a danger to them. It took time, but Liza kept close. A few times she placed a hand on his shoulder and they both paused, listening to the whistling wind as daylight flirted with the horizon.

Finally, he found one of the caves he'd had in mind. He no longer needed the penlight in the hazy dawn. He nodded toward the opening, watching Liza's face recoil.

But her body didn't.

"What if something's inside?"

Jamison picked up a few rocks from the ground and threw them as far into the cave as he could, even though it made the pain in his arm sing.

He listened intently for the sounds of life but didn't hear any. With a shrug, he climbed for the opening. When he reached it, he flipped on his headlamp, which he'd retrieved back when they'd fought off the scouts. Then he unholstered his gun and pulled it into his hand. He used the other hand to give him balance as he began to move inside.

He used the beam of his lamp to sweep the area, looking for any sign of a serious threat—bones or scat. A few bats fluttered by his head, deeper into the cave, but there was no sign of a big predator that might attack.

"I don't want to do this. I don't want to do this," Liza chanted, over and over, the farther they crept into the cave. But that was the thing about Liza. She might chant that for the next twenty-four hours straight, but here she was. Doing it anyway.

"Jamison. They could surround us. They could… There are *so* many possibilities."

"There are, but I have a bit of an ace in the hole, so to speak." Satisfied they'd moved deep enough into the cave, he eased himself to the rocky ground, grateful for the rest even if it was cold and damp. He pulled the item he'd lifted off the man he'd fought.

"You have their *walkie!*" She reached out to grab it, but he kept it out of reach.

"Palmed it off the guy I fought. We should be able to hear everything they're doing out there."

"And you're just telling me this *now*? Why haven't we been listening to it this whole time?" She hadn't sat, was stooped over, but still managed to look imperious and demanding, with her hands on her hips in this dim little cave.

"We couldn't use it until we were for sure out of hearing range," he said, rubbing at the ache in his chest that swept over him. An ache that had nothing to do with his injuries and everything to do with her.

Because fifteen years could sweep between them, but it didn't seem to change *this*. A wave of affection, mixed with desire and something like awe. He could be mad at her, he could think she'd betrayed him—chosen the Sons over him—but she was still here and standing. Anyone who survived that long in the Sons and still wanted to do something good and right had to be nearly superhuman.

Thoughts like that would get him into trouble—betrayed again, dead possibly—and yet he was getting worse and worse at fighting them away.

"We might be out of walkie range," she said, frowning at the device.

"We might be, but I doubt the Sons use these if they don't have good range." He switched it on. "Here goes nothing."

LIZA HELD HER BREATH. There was nothing but the low hum of static. She closed her eyes. Worthless.

But when she opened her eyes, her beam of light shone on Jamison's battered face. More to worry about in the here and now.

She dropped her pack and rummaged through it. She pulled out a windbreaker, hoping it was waterproof, and kneeled on it. Then she got out any first aid supplies she could find, along with a bottle of water.

"Drink that. Don't waste it on me."

"Don't be stupid." It was true they didn't know how long they'd be out here, and water would become a commodity they simply couldn't take for granted. But neither could infection—and his face was dirty and cut to pieces.

She found a cotton T-shirt in his pack and ripped it in half before wetting one half to use as a washcloth to clean his face.

He scowled at her and he didn't look the same as he had fifteen years ago. He was harder, and not as lean as he'd been at twenty-two. Time and age had packed muscles on. The sun had dug faint lines around his eyes and mouth—just a hint of age.

She supposed she had a few lines of her own that hadn't been there when she'd been twenty. She wasn't as lean, either—but instead of firm muscle, there were spots of softness to her.

Of course, going hungry more often than not hadn't exactly packed on the pounds Carlee had always been so worried about.

Carlee. Just thinking about her hurt. Reminded Liza of the last time she'd seen Gigi.

Mommy's gone. The bad men hurt her. She couldn't see. Her eyes were open, but she couldn't see.

Liza blew out a breath and stared at the man before her. He eyed her warily, but there was something more than caution in that gaze. She was reminded of that moment when she'd told him he'd only hate himself.

Because he might still feel the echoes of those old…emotions between them, but he wasn't about to wade down that same path. Save her. Love her. Promise to protect always.

No, she'd blown that chance to pieces.

She swallowed at *everything* that whirled around inside her and leaned forward and began to wash the dirt off his face, trying to be gentle with his injuries. He didn't hiss out in pain, but she could feel the tension in his body as he fought off those responses to pain.

Without fully realizing it, she murmured encouraging words as she used the disinfectant in the kit, then bandaged up what cuts she could, touching his rough skin, the bristle of his whiskers, the bridge of his sharp nose she'd always thought was *noble*.

When had she ever been foolish enough to think about the shape of someone's nose and ascribe it to nobility?

She finished, still studying him. His complexion had grayed, but his eyes were alert and not so wary anymore. No, heat all but cracked from them. An awareness. Because they'd been skin to skin and were too close, breathing too much of the same air.

Time couldn't erase what their bodies had once found in each other.

She tried to remind herself he would have loved other women over the course of fifteen years. Probably forgotten what it was like to press his lips to hers. To fill her with that ridiculous desperation only teenagers ever truly felt. Because even in the harsh world they'd grown up in, they'd still just been teenagers. Hormones and recklessness and a belief—if not in their own immortality—in their ability to outwit and survive anything thrown at them.

Because for a few short, sweet years they had survived all this. Escaped and had their whole lives of freedom ahead of them.

She was older now, had seen too much, lost too much, to have that simple, joyous belief anymore.

It settled in her, a heavy weight. The loss, not just of him but of that feeling, and all she could do was lean forward and press her forehead to his shoulder.

When his arm came around her, a silent, strong

comfort, she gave in to the sobs she'd been fighting for weeks.

"Sleep," he whispered, pulling her head down, until she was somehow cradled in his lap, curled up in a ball. He stroked her hair as her sobs subsided. Dried her cheeks. Exhaustion cloaked her like a blanket and she fell into a deep sleep.

Where she dreamed of the dead.

Chapter Eleven

Jamison hadn't meant to fall asleep, but he could hardly beat himself up over it. They'd hiked all night and exhaustion could only be fought for so long.

He opened his eyes, frowning at the fact Liza wasn't still curled up against him and sleeping as though she felt completely safe with him.

Something inside him had cracked open into a million pieces or *something*, and when he'd fallen into a sleep he'd tried to fight off, he'd dreamed of something he couldn't ever remember dreaming about or even feeling.

True peace.

Which was crazy. As long as the Sons existed, and his father was alive, there was no peace to be found. Jamison was practical enough not to believe in perfect worlds where he defeated both.

But maybe he could defeat one and slow down the other—at best.

He looked up to find Liza on the other side of the narrow cave not a few feet from him, watching him.

All traces of vulnerability were gone and she chewed on a protein bar.

It irritated him that she'd woken up first and moved off him without him waking up. He should be more in tune with his surroundings. But he couldn't lean into that anger because they had more important things to deal with.

He watched her as she grabbed another bar and tossed it at him. He caught it but didn't stop staring.

She was the key to something. Something inside him. Something he'd been waiting for...all these years.

He didn't believe in fate or true love or any of the things either could *mean*, but here he was.

"You okay, champ?"

Nope. "Anything on the two-way?"

"Not that I've heard, but I haven't been awake much longer than you."

That was some comfort. Perhaps he'd woken because she'd gotten up and off him, and it had just taken a few minutes to jolt into clarity. Jamison looked at his watch. It was still before noon—so he'd slept about five hours. It could be they'd hiked far enough to be out of range. It could be that the search party—if they'd figured out their scouts had been taken out—had gone the wrong direction.

"Probably a good sign," he decided, trying to be hopeful though it wasn't his natural inclination.

"Unless they noted the missing walkie and changed the frequency," Liza pointed out.

"Lucky for us, we can test out that theory." He

held out a hand, waiting for her to toss the handheld at him, but she didn't.

"You talk in your sleep," she said instead, dark eyes watching him with something he wasn't sure he'd be able to name if he lived to be a very old man.

Since he vaguely remembered his dreams, all about her, he stiffened, but he wouldn't let himself shift and give in to how exposed he felt. "Do I?" he replied blandly. "Anything interesting?"

"I guess it depends on who you were muttering about."

"I wouldn't know. I don't remember my dreams."

She made a considering sound but didn't comment further. He unwrapped the protein bar and took an unsatisfactory bite. "Change the channels. Give each one about ten minutes and see if we pick up on anything."

He reached for his pack, wincing at the way his body had stiffened over the course of their nap. Everything ached or was too stiff. Was he thirty-seven or ninety-seven? He stretched a bit, pulling his bottle of water out and taking a drink. Then he tried to roll the kinks out of his neck as he went to his pocket for the map.

But it wasn't there. There was a moment of blind panic before he remembered Liza had it. Trying to hide the galloping of his heartbeat, he took a slow, deliberate breath and kept his gaze on the protein bar until he calmed that unnecessary jolt.

"Map?" he finally asked casually, if he did say so himself.

She pulled the square of paper from her pocket. "This isn't going to hold up through much more of this." Instead of handing it to him like he would have preferred, she unfolded it on her own lap. "What is all this, by the way? Because these marks are something more than just what's been going on the past few days."

He shrugged. "Just a map."

"No. It's a map with a code. Spill it, Jamison."

"Why?"

She looked up from the map, met his gaze. "Because we're in this together."

She didn't say *always*, but it seemed to hang in the air between them. Whatever they were, whoever they were, *always* seemed just about right.

Maybe that was why the hurt from her disappearing all those years ago had never healed, just left a jagged edge he'd never been able to set aside for any other woman.

Liza was his always, whether she was with him or not. Whether he wanted her to be or not.

Too vulnerable a thought and he'd rather discuss what they needed to focus on. "I've kept track over the years. Even after we—I got out, if I heard of something related to the Sons, I marked it. Dead bodies are an X. The hashtags represent petty crime. Camps are squares. Unexplained disappearances I thought might relate back to the Sons are circles— in the margins if there were no known last whereabouts."

She blinked and looked back down at the map.

"You kept *track*? All these years you kept track and never…"

He knew what she meant to say before she trailed off. Knew because he was always wondering what more he could have done. But having her say it burned. "Never what?" he demanded.

"Did anything." She shook her head, raising her gaze from the map to him. "You knew all this was going on and you never did anything." She looked at him as if he'd morphed before her very eyes into a villain.

Her words weren't true, but that look hurt. Injured enough that he wouldn't defend himself. Why bother? She wanted to believe he was the ultimate bad guy—what did it matter?

He really didn't want it to matter. There was no point in trying to explain *anything* to her. But his mouth always had a mind of its own around her.

"Brady, Gage and Tucker work for the Valiant County Sheriff's Department, just like me. I have contacts in county departments across South Dakota. I put pressure where I could on those cases. So did they. We've done what we can."

But he was just one man—not a gang or a federal agency. There was only so much he could do within the confines of the law. It had never felt like a failure—even when the law handcuffed him—until Liza had looked at him with that hurt and horrified expression.

"Hand me the map," he said roughly.

She shook her head and grabbed her pack, rifling

through it until she pulled out a pen. She made a few of her own marks, then tossed the map at him.

He scanned the map, noticed her big black X about fifteen miles north of Flynn.

"You know that's where Carlee was murdered?"

"No, not for sure. My father has some kind of house in that area—I don't have an exact location but it's somewhere there. You know how he always liked to keep a separate place. A step above. Keep his family out of reach so he could be their only tormentor. I don't know where else he would have killed Carlee that Gigi would have been able to witness it."

He nodded, a new idea occurring to him. He'd figured west made the most sense in terms of transportation, but if Liza's father was the point man on the trafficking...

"What's around the cabin? Give me details."

Liza shook her head. "I don't know."

Irritated that even now she'd keep things from him, he didn't bother to hide the sharpness in his tone. "Liza."

"Trust me. I wasn't allowed within miles. Gigi told me a few things, but nothing that will help us find it. They may have let me back in the Sons, but I wasn't trusted. Not in all those years. I'm the Mariah of this generation, just hoping my turn to die wasn't until after I'd helped my sisters."

Mariah. He remembered a woman in her forties. Tough and always mouthing off and getting knocked around when she did it to the wrong person. It never stopped her, and for the longest time Jamison and

Liza had wondered why she got to live. No one else showed disrespect like that and got to stay—and keep breathing.

She'd even helped Jamison once, when he'd been getting Tucker out. He'd been about to get caught, and she'd created a diversion.

A year later, she'd been used—very much against her will—as a suicide bomber that had allowed the Sons to interfere with a prisoner transport and get one of their men back from the feds.

Because the true danger of the Sons, at least under his father's leadership, was that they were patient. They were smart. They didn't expend anyone until their usefulness had been completely wrung out.

Jamison supposed that was part of the reason for his own freedom the past fifteen years. Dad was waiting for the time he'd be most useful, and he could wait a very, very long time.

Maybe this was what they should have done, all along. Force Ace's hand. Take the power back. Be the ones to move, just like they'd been when Jamison had gotten them all out.

Regardless, here he was. "What if it's here? At your father's place or close—close enough Carlee caught wind. The Sons don't kill without planning, but if Gigi witnessed Carlee's death or just her *being* dead, it wasn't planned—or not very well. I never saw my mother. She was there one day. Gone the next."

Something like sympathy softened Liza's expression, so he pushed on because he didn't want any of her sympathy.

"Your father did always like his place on the hill, like you said, but fifteen miles? That's an awful lot for the second in command. Ace wouldn't be good with that unless there was a reason."

"That's… Yeah, that could be."

"It would also explain why we're not getting any hits on the two-way. We've gone west. If they're protecting your father or the trafficking, they might have gone north."

She nodded, let out a little huff, not in relief but maybe determination. She met his gaze. "So, I guess we're headed north."

THEY LET THE afternoon wear on while they waited in the cave. They took turns switching the dials on the two-way, listening for clues or hints, but every channel was low-level static.

As sunset crept closer, they began to prepare to leave. Jamison thought that no walkie activity meant they'd be safe to start before dark fully descended, and Liza was glad to get *some* daylight hiking in before the stumbling, panic-inducing night trek.

Now they had a clear target. She couldn't entertain thoughts that Jamison might be off base. He had to be right, and they had to be heading for Gigi.

She tried not to think about how it led straight to her father.

They packed up the gear in silence. Jamison shoved some trail mix at her, and his bottle of water.

Since she didn't want to break the silence and argue, she ate and drank as much as her churning stomach could handle.

She insisted on checking his face and bandages, reapplying a few. Of course, that only meant he insisted on changing her bandage, which meant mostly removing her pants.

She was getting a little tired of feeling his hands on her skin while he changed her bandage with absolutely no hint that it might affect him in any way.

She could be anyone. A stranger. One of his brothers. He'd bandage them all with the same gentle detachment. Actually, he'd be rougher with his brothers, because he cared about them. He'd be angry they'd been hurt.

She was as good as a stranger.

More than that she was an idiot for letting her mind go in these pointless circles when her sister was in grave danger. But Jamison had found a lead—a good one, if her instincts were on track like his.

She hissed a little when he used a disinfectant wipe against her wound, but he was quick with it and was almost immediately spreading the soft, cool bandage over the stitches.

His hands were rough—likely from work he did at the ranch to help out Dev and Grandma Pauline. He might live in Bonesteel, a good forty-five minutes away from the ranch, but Jamison would lend whatever help he could.

Help. It was his core. He'd kept track of things the Sons had done, and as much as she'd felt a moment of betrayal, it hadn't lasted. He'd used his law enforcement influence to try to right crimes committed by the Sons.

He hadn't explained what the check marks on the map had meant, but she knew. Those were cases where he'd actually been instrumental in getting an arrest made. She didn't recognize all of them, but Lyle Pearce had been arrested and convicted of murder three years ago—much to her father and Ace Wyatt's fury—which was most definitely Jamison's X and check mark just west of Bonesteel.

He hadn't forgotten, hadn't let it all go like he pretended. She had to wonder if Ace knew that—and was keeping the same kind of tabs for every time his son interfered.

She swallowed at the fear. It was one thing when she'd known she was the Mariah—that she could at any point be used for the Sons' ends and die—but it was another to think of just how much hatred Ace might have built up against his eldest son. More than she'd anticipated.

Which made this all the more dangerous for Jamison. Her heart and gut twisted and she wanted to say something as he finished with the bandage, but she couldn't.

He was still crouched at her feet, spreading the new bandage over her leg, his calloused fingers grazing across the skin just outside the bandage's reach.

His gaze lifted, heated. As he stood, he kept her gaze—and lifted her pants, the very tips of his fingers brushing along her skin as he did so. She held her breath, his heated gaze melting everything inside her, including the fear.

Because Jamison had always been her safe place—and she'd always wanted safe as much as her body had wanted his.

Now was not the time to give in, but she was drowning in all that sparked between them and deep inside her. He reached his full height, inches above her own, and she leaned toward him even as her brain told her it was a mistake.

She got up on her tiptoes and pressed her body against his. It matched, just the same as it always had. They matched, heart, soul, body. She gave herself time to watch him, to wait for some inkling he felt it, too.

He showed no signs of reaction. He held himself still, and his eyes remained cool. Which made something inside her crack in half—perhaps her sanity—because in the next moment she pressed her mouth to his, his lack of response be damned.

He didn't balk like she'd expected. He didn't push her away. He let her kiss him. And somehow, second by second, inch by inch, he sank into the kiss. Softening, reacting, taking. It was such a surprise she threw herself into it wholly.

The kiss ignited—not like in the old days, with sparks of desperation and joy. This was different—deeper and more complex. Not just spark, but full-on explosion from the inside out. It was joy and need but also betrayal and confusion. It was hope and it was cynicism. It was everything they were and had been in their fifteen years apart.

But at its core the kiss was *them*—whatever had brought them together as friends when they'd been kids, whatever had bloomed between them as they'd learned what the opposite sex had to offer. It was their hearts, entwined still, after all these years— because for whatever reason, they were made for each other and could never bend or twist to be some-one else's.

He was the only man she'd ever wanted, the only man she'd ever willingly touched intimately, and there was some *relief* that fifteen years hadn't changed that.

But the reprieve swirled with the sadness of real-ity. This world of theirs dulled the edges of euphoria. Yet she was still breathless, boneless maybe, throw-ing herself and her heart into this whirlwind of a kiss.

He wrapped his arms around her, strong and cer-tain. He kissed her with *intention*, not just despera-tion. As if there was some way they could erase all those old hurts and start something new and pur-poseful.

But too few moments later, he pushed her away. Slowly and carefully, but a clear push nonetheless.

Silence and heat swirled around them in the low light of the cave. Her body pulsed with an electricity she'd nearly forgotten existed, because no one but Jamison had ever made her feel outside herself—just sensation and heart with no concern for the physi-cal here and now.

It hardly mattered. It was a pointless kiss and he'd pushed her away, no matter what she felt.

It had been a waste of time at best, though it lingered inside her. She meant to give him a sassy smile and an offhand remark, but she was too steeped in feeling to manage it. "I just had to know if it was all still there," she whispered. The truth—in all its pointless glory.

His gaze was enigmatic and impossible to read—or maybe she didn't want to read it. Maybe she didn't want to know what he was feeling. His words certainly didn't give much away.

"I guess it is."

But it *was* an admission. Not exactly a timely one. "Not really the time to figure that out."

He kept watching her and giving her no clue as to how he felt. "Not especially."

"We should go." She made a move for the outside world, but Jamison's hand was still on her arm, and it held firm.

She thought he might kiss her again—hoped, maybe. But he only watched, searched. There was something very nearly vulnerable in his eyes, so she stood still before it and let him find what he sought.

"Was it me?" he asked, his voice a harsh rasp. "I was too…overbearing. A different version of them. You had to run away from—"

She didn't need an explanation to know he was talking about her leaving, to be horrified he'd blame himself. "Oh, Jamison. God. *No*. No, I wanted to *be* you. Save my sisters like you'd saved your brothers.

I wanted to prove I was as good as you." It hit her then what she'd never fully allowed herself to admit. "I never could."

He flinched, as though the words were a slap. Then he let her go. "I guess it doesn't matter."

She'd thought that. That he'd never understand. That fifteen years was too long, but here in this moment she wondered.

Unfortunately, now was most definitely not the time to figure it out. "We should go," she repeated. If they didn't, what other emotional pain would they bring up to compete with the physical pain of their injuries?

"I'll exit first, search a little, then you. We've got a long walk."

Yes, they had a long, *long* way to go.

Chapter Twelve

It was another beautiful sunset streaking across the sky as they marched silently toward their target. Jamison could remember nights when they'd still been with the Sons, when he and Liza would hike some hill or rock outcropping, depending on where their camp had been, and watch the sunset.

She used to say sunsets held such promise—for a new day. He'd always responded that, technically, that happened with sunrises.

Every time she'd grin at him and say, *Yeah, but who wants to get up that early?*

He'd refused to touch her when they'd been in the Sons. It would have been a violation of what he was trying to do, the man he wanted to be. The first time she'd kissed him, he'd lectured her on proper behavior even as his heart had beaten so hard against his chest he thought it'd break through.

He could still remember the careless smirk she'd flashed him in the moonlight. How he'd wanted to wallow in it, and in her. How close he'd been to breaking his own vow to himself over a little kiss and a careless smile.

Hell. Now was not the time to wander down memory lane—especially the happier side to it.

If he was where he thought they were, and they didn't run into any problems, and he didn't get turned around and lost, Jamison thought they could be close to Liza's father's place by dawn.

So, they walked. They didn't talk much. Every once in a while they'd take a rest, a few sips of water and have a snack. They'd go through the channels on the two-way and listen for anything.

Then they'd be back on their feet before too long, using headlamps to see in the inky dark. The lights made Jamison nervous, as did the fact they'd decided to keep the two-way on low despite the fact the sound might tip off someone searching for them.

They were risks they'd have to take to mitigate the risks of getting lost or more hurt in the dark.

When Jamison thought they were getting close, he had Liza shut off the handheld and her lamp. They walked just by his light for a while. The landscape had morphed. They were still hiking through rocky outcroppings, but now many of the rocks were surrounded by forest.

The trees were good cover for the light, and a good place to rest as dawn began to threaten.

Liza yawned, and he fought off one of his own.

"We should take a break."

Liza all but collapsed on a patch of grass, heaving out a sigh of relief. "Thank God."

"Not much of one. I think we're close. What do you think?"

She looked around the dark, shadowy woods. "I don't know. I really don't."

Jamison took a seat next to her and pulled out his map and penlight. He switched off his headlamp. He studied the map in the small circle of light, the geological features mixed with his own markings, which, amid the trail of crime, included landmarks that only meant anything to Jamison himself.

He pointed to the X she'd made that signified Carlee, then drew his finger a short distance south. "I think we're about here. Do you have any idea how big the place is?"

"I asked Gigi what it looked like. What she described sounded like a cabin—a decent one. She mentioned a fireplace and Carlee cooking before it happened. Baking brownies. Sounded like they had modern conveniences. When I asked her about outside, Gigi said she had a playground—swings, a slide."

"So, a nice place, likely. Bigger rather than smaller."

"Maybe, but Gigi didn't mention anything about anyone else. Just her and Carlee and my father. If they were trafficking under her nose, she would have mentioned other people."

"It could be more like a compound, and Gigi and Carlee were supposed to stay in the house. I have to believe if your father did something that drastic with a witness who wouldn't know to be quiet, Carlee had to be close. Maybe something not in the house, but near it."

"She mentioned horses," Liza said, almost to herself. "I'd forgotten that because it wasn't when we were talking about Carlee. It was before. Gigi said she missed her horse. At first I thought she was talking about a stuffed animal or something."

"Stables. Horses. That's not like the Sons." They were mobile, nomads. But things had changed. Liza had told him that and he needed to stop being surprised by it.

"No, it isn't. Your father could move anything he has in the snap of a finger, but it seems like my father was settling in for good."

"How did you get to Gigi after Carlee was dead?"

"I didn't know Carlee was dead yet. No one did— at least no one had told me. I think I would have heard, though. I think if anyone else knew, they would have made sure to tell me—not out of loyalty, mind you, but because it would have been a way to make me feel bad."

At Jamison's outraged look, she shrugged. "I'm the Mariah, remember? Take shots at me as long as they don't interfere with my potential use. It would have been a shot. So, I think they were keeping it quiet."

"So, how did Gigi tell you?"

"Dad and Carlee and Gigi would come into the main camp about once a week. I tried to keep tabs on Gigi—be where she was when she was in camp. Talk to Carlee, plant the seeds of escape. The day Gigi told me, Dad had come in to meet with your father like he normally did, but Carlee wasn't with

Loyal Readers
FREE BOOKS Voucher

We're giving away

THOUSANDS of FREE BOOKS

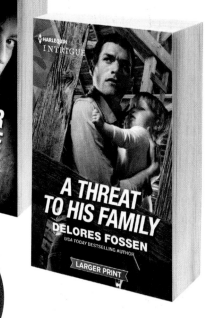

Get 2
FREE FABULOUS BOOKS
You Love!

To thank you for being a loyal reader we'd like to send you 2 FREE BOOKS, absolutely free.

Just write "YES" on the Loyal Reader Voucher and we'll send you 2 Free Books and 2 Free Mystery Gifts, altogether worth over $20, as a way of saying thank you for being a loyal reader.

We are so glad you love the books as much as we do and can't wait to send you great new books.

So don't miss out, return your Loyal Reader Voucher Today!

Pam Powers

LOYAL READER
FREE BOOKS VOUCHER

YES! I Love Reading, please send me 2 FREE BOOKS and 2 FREE Mystery Gifts.

Just write in "YES" on the dotted line below then return this card today and we'll send your free books & gifts asap!

➡ _ YES _ ⬅

Which do you prefer?

☐ **I prefer Regular-Print**
182/382 HDL GNS4

☐ **I prefer Larger-Print**
199/399 HDL GNS4

FIRST NAME	LAST NAME

ADDRESS

APT.#   CITY

STATE/PROV.   ZIP/POSTAL CODE

him. He gave Gigi to a couple of the teenage girls to watch after her while he conducted business. It was a nice day, so they were letting her throw rocks in the pond. The girls watching her were too busy on their phones to notice or care that I was talking to her. I thought. Maybe they told Dad after, I don't know. But I didn't expect Gigi to tell me all that, either."

"How many days between Gigi telling you and you coming to me in Bonesteel?"

"Three. I thought I was being sneaky. I followed them—not back to wherever Dad is living because he has too many guards, but I went as far down that path as I thought was safe. Then every time they came back into camp that way, I'd follow and try to find a time to get Gigi alone."

"How many times did you succeed?"

"Once after the first time. I didn't want to upset her or draw attention, so it was hard. The day I came to Bonesteel…Gigi wasn't there. Dad came to town without her. I don't know if he'd heard what we were talking about last time, but I knew if I stayed we'd both be hurt. I knew I needed help. So, that's when I came to you."

That shouldn't fill him with warmth, satisfy some rough edges inside him. But it did, as pathetic as that made him.

"Sleep. I'll keep watch." They didn't have much time before daylight would make things more dangerous, but she needed to rest.

She eyed him in the dark. "Are you sure?"

"Yeah."

When she tried to position herself against a tree, he rolled his eyes. "Come here," he said, the words coming out more as a sharp order than he'd intended. He took her arm and pulled until she was close enough to use him as a pillow.

She looked up at him for a fathomless second, all those old pulls urging him forward, the memory of the kiss in the cave urging him forward.

But Liza only sighed and leaned her head onto his shoulder, using him as the pillow he was meant to be.

He used the map and the penlight to keep him awake. One arm around a sleeping Liza meant he spread the map out on the ground at his other side, and used his hand to hold the penlight.

He studied and searched and considered different routes. As light began to dawn, he turned off the penlight and pulled out the two-way handheld and turned the volume low and to its original channel.

Liza slept soundly. He watched, a little too long, as the brightening golden light haloed her features. He'd convinced himself all of what he felt in this moment had been gone. He'd been so sure he'd erased her from his mind and his heart after fifteen years.

But in some ways it felt like no time had passed. Here she was, right where she belonged. With him.

He scrubbed his free hand over his face and stopped on a dime when he caught sight of movement in the trees.

Someone, or *someones*, was out there. He could make out one figure—who didn't seem worried about hiding his presence.

Something about the way the figure moved was…familiar. Jamison held very still, watching the stranger, though he itched to look at Liza to make sure she was still asleep.

He slowly, slowly moved his hand toward his weapon. The figure in the distance did the same.

Liza shifted and Jamison immediately whispered a command to be silent. She stilled in his lap as his hand curled over the butt of his gun.

The figure moved a little closer, still too far away. But their gazes met and held, Jamison was sure of that.

"Cody?" He hadn't realized he'd muttered it out loud until Liza responded.

"Your brother?" Liza whispered.

"I don't…" But those were his brother's eyes, his brother's moves. The man simply stood there, off in the distance, but why would Jamison think it was Cody if it wasn't? Maybe he only saw his youngest brother at Christmas, and the occasional Easter Sunday, but that was Cody.

"Don't move," Jamison instructed Liza, slowly sliding out from under her.

He ignored her whispered arguments and moved toward the man. The man was armed, but not aiming a weapon in Jamison's direction.

Because it was his brother. As Jamison approached, Cody held his finger to his lips, nodded to the walkie on his hip. One that looked suspiciously like the one Jamison had in his pack. But it couldn't be possible Cody was *with* the Sons. He'd probably come across it just as Jamison had come across his.

But his brother didn't look harmed in any way, or even tired like he'd been hiking around all night.

Still, when Cody took Jamison's hand and lifted it, Jamison didn't fight him off or even get in a stance that might make him ready for attack.

This was his brother. His *baby* brother. Jamison had gotten Cody out of the Sons when Cody had been just shy of seven—before Cody had had to go through the seven-nights-alone "man" ritual. Jamison considered it his greatest success. Cody had lived with Grandma Pauline for the longest period of time. He'd gone to college. Jamison hadn't been able to save him from all memory of being in the Sons, but a lot of the worst parts.

Cody couldn't be with the Sons. Jamison wouldn't believe it.

He realized, belatedly, Cody was tapping his finger against Jamison's palm. It took Jamison a few times to realize Cody was using Morse code.

Go.

Jamison opened his mouth to respond, but Cody shook his head and brought his finger to his lips again.

So, Jamison tapped out his response on his brother's palm, perhaps more firmly than necessary.

No.

You have to.

No.

Not safe.

No.

Can't protect you.

Don't need to.

Cody made a sound of frustration and then looked around the woods.

Don't ruin this. Then his brother dropped Jamison's hand and melted into the woods.

Jamison wasn't sure how long he stood there after Cody had disappeared. It felt like a dream, or like he'd been visited by a ghost. The incident certainly gave him far more questions than it could ever answer.

Ruin *what*, most of all.

Eventually he turned, listening intently for the sounds of anyone else. But there was only him and Liza in the forest.

"What on earth was that?" she demanded when he returned.

Jamison stared out into the empty woods. "I wish I knew."

As JAMISON RELATED his exchange with Cody, Liza tried to choke down another disgusting protein bar. Fainting here like she had back in Bonesteel was a death sentence for both of them, but, boy, did she wish she had anything else to eat.

"He had a walkie, just like the one we have?" she asked, swallowing down a gummy bite.

"He had a walkie. If it was like the one we have, it would have been going off. He had it on."

"Ours hasn't been going off," Liza pointed out. She didn't want to say it, but that was a sympathy she didn't have room for right now. "You have to admit, it looks like he's with the Sons."

"Did you hear any whispers about that?" Jamison demanded.

"No, but—"

"Then he's not," he returned firmly and with completely certainty. "That news would spread like wildfire. If you didn't know—it's not possible."

She *almost* felt sorry for him, but she had to say it. "Unless it's Ace's secret."

Jamison shook his head and closed his backpack with more force than necessary. "There'd be no reason for Ace to keep Cody a secret. He'd crow from dusk till dawn about getting one of us back."

"Unless there's absolutely a reason for him to keep it a secret—one of Ace's many reasons and plans."

"Cody warned me off, Liza. The Sons don't do that."

She wanted to let it go, but they were walking straight into the lion's den here. She couldn't ignore what was possible. "Sure, mostly. But it would make sense if Cody had a soft spot for you. He might be with the Sons and still not want to tangle with anything that involved hurting *you*."

"It's not possible."

"Because you don't want it to be or because it's really not?"

He whipped his gaze to hers, furious. She might have been afraid of that fury, or even offended by it, but she understood that Cody joining the Sons would be worse than *anything* for Jamison. Worse than her leaving all those years ago. Worse than the Sons hurting Jamison himself.

One of his brothers—his youngest brother, whom he'd saved at the youngest age. It'd kill Jamison to consider Cody might have gone back.

But it was *possible*, and kill him or not, she had to be rational enough to accept that possibility. "Whatever he is, he's not going to hurt you. So he says, but that doesn't mean he won't tip some people off to our whereabouts." *Especially mine.*

"I will not, under any circumstances, consider my brother is part of the Sons," he said, his voice not just cold but frigid and fierce. Icicles piercing their target. "Now. We move toward where we think your father's place might be."

She wouldn't get through to him about Cody when he was that angry, so she focused on her other concerns. "In broad daylight?"

"Did you have a better idea, Liza? I don't see any caves or good enough cover. Please, tell me, what *should* we do?"

"Well, you could stop taking your irritation out on me. It's not my fault your brother might have gone into the Sons."

Whatever storms ignited inside him, he kept a calm lid on them. But she could see all that *pain* brewing. "So, it's my fault, then."

Which was not stated as a question—which irritated *her*. "Do you ever listen to anyone besides yourself? Are you so self-absorbed you think you're the cause of everything?"

He started striding toward some point only he knew. "No," he said firmly, but it was hardly with the same vehemence he'd turned on her.

Liza sighed and trudged after him, but she couldn't let it go—much as she wished she could. "Oh, just us, then? You're responsible for us because we're so weak and stupid and—"

He whirled on her, and that calm lid was bubbling over into fury. "I *saved* you. Both of you. So, explain to me, if you both went back, what went wrong?"

He just about broke her heart. Because no, it wasn't fury bubbling over, it was fear. It was worry and guilt. She knew they didn't have time for the healing of old wounds, but she couldn't let that one bleed out while they walked. So, she took his face in her hands, resting her palms against his cheeks. "Not you, honey. What went wrong was never you."

"So, what was it?" He lifted his hands to her wrists as if he was going to pull her hands away, but in the end he just rested them there. She thought he meant the question to be rhetorical, but it hung there.

"We don't all know how to be good," she said, wishing she knew how to explain all the things he couldn't understand. Because he *was* good. It was some inherent thing inside him. "We don't all know how to want what's good—or keep it. It isn't in us like it's in you. Not all of us. That's not your failing, Jamison."

His eyebrows drew together, that edgy fury softening. "I don't think you can call it your own, either. Not how we grew up."

It wasn't the time to smile, but her lips curved anyway. "Oh, Jamison. How did you turn out so good? I'll never know. You don't need to absolve me. I know what I am."

"Do you?"

For a second, that simple question made her wonder. But no. She knew. "I wanted to be you, but I couldn't save Marci. Now I'll never save Carlee. Gigi is my last hope to do any kind of good for my sisters."

"You never had to be me. You said it yourself. It's different for men and women in there. It's different for the sons of Ace Wyatt than the daughter of Tony Dean. Always has been and always will be. Whatever you couldn't do isn't a failure."

No, there was no time to heal old wounds, but that soothed some. Even as she tried to fight the warm wave of relief away. She didn't need him to tell her what it was or how it was different. He did not and could not change the failure she'd had with Marci and Carlee.

But her heart felt less bruised no matter what her brain tried to tell it.

"Do you ever say that to yourself, Jamison? Or is everything your failure?"

"We should walk," he said, his voice still rough.

Liza nodded, though for another few seconds they stood there in the still woods, her hands on his face and his hands on her wrists.

A good man. Hard to let go. Older and wiser, it was harder to think she had to be noble and let him be that good man without her.

Now was not the time. He dropped his hands and she dropped hers, and then they set out for another hike. She tried not to think about her throbbing feet, her aching wound or that look on Jamison's face that caused a deep pain at the center of her chest.

After walking awhile, the sun climbing higher in the sky and making Liza more and more nervous they'd be seen and caught, Jamison held up his arm and stopped.

Slowly, he pulled his gun out of his holster and then nodded at her to get out the gun he'd given her. She did so, trying to be as quiet as possible as she shifted the contents of her pack.

When Jamison stepped forward, it was into a clearing. She realized he hadn't seen a direct threat, but they were treading on dangerous ground.

A small rustic-looking cabin sat in the middle of a small clearing in a thicket of a variety of trees. Leaves were lumped in random piles, likely dropped off by the wind. The windows were dark with grime where they weren't shattered by unknown forces. It looked deserted, old and not well kept.

But looks could be deceiving.

It wasn't her father's place that Gigi had described, and if it was held by the Sons, no doubt she and Jamison would already be dead or threatened.

She followed Jamison, gun in hand, watching the woods and the black windows as they moved around the clearing in a broad circle, then a smaller one.

She wasn't the best shot, especially when she was nervous, but she knew how to work a gun, and hopefully that amounted to something. Well, hopefully she didn't have to shoot at all.

The outside looked deserted—for a rather long time. There weren't footprints or signs anything had been disturbed. There was no sight or sound of anyone. When they completed another, even smaller circle, Jamison nodded at the door. "Let's see what we've got."

Liza nodded. They moved, close enough to be one. Jamison reached out and turned the knob. It squeaked and groaned, but it turned and the door pushed open.

Jamison led with the gun, slowly pushing the door more and more open until sunlight spilled into the dim, dusty interior.

She followed Jamison close all the way through the cabin, searching the meager cabinets and closets and nooks and crannies. Some furniture that looked abandoned, but mostly just dust and grime, and a few signs of animal life.

"Someone's been here recently, but they didn't want anyone to know it," Jamison said, slowly lowering his gun.

Liza did the same with her gun, but frowned at the surroundings. It didn't look like anyone had been here in decades to her. "How can you tell?"

"The windows aren't as dusty as the counters. Someone's opened them and then brushed off their prints or tracks in the dust. That chair there—you can see the track in the dust where it's been moved."

"Could be animals."

"It's not. But whoever was here isn't anymore. Which is good news for us."

"How? If someone's been here, they could come back."

"They could, but they didn't leave anything behind, so I think we're safe there. We can rest here while we wait for nightfall."

"And what happens at nightfall?"

"We try to find your father's place. Ideally we do and can case it and formulate a plan of rescue."

"Just the two of us?"

"You know, it could be Cody was here trying to do the same thing we are."

Liza figured it was better to agree with him than keep mounting arguments. She wasn't so sure about Cody Wyatt, but Jamison probably knew his brother better than she did. "It could be."

"I know you don't believe me."

"I don't have to, Jamison. Just like I don't need you to believe me that I think he's with the Sons. We can think different things and still do everything we've got to do."

He scrubbed a hand over his face, then winced at the pain it must have caused his injuries from his previous scuffle. "Yeah." He blew out a breath, looking around the cabin. "We should rest."

Liza looked dubiously at the musty old mattress in the corner. It was better than a cave, she supposed. She inched onto it, wrinkling her nose. Definitely smelly and dusty.

"Here," Jamison muttered. He shrugged off his

pack and then pulled out a pouch. He untied it and slowly unraveled what became a blanket.

"Well, aren't you handy."

"Something like that." He spread out the blanket, waited for her to sit down and then took a seat next to her.

She looked at him. The weight of the world on his shoulders, as it always was. The battle light that never tired no matter how much his body did. Cuts and bruises across his face that he acted as if didn't even exist, though they had to hurt. Constantly.

She reached out and brushed her fingers across his unmarred temple, like she used to do when she was swamped with love for a boy who was way too good for her. Way too good for the world he'd been stuck in. Slowly, he turned his head and met her gaze.

There were some things just as dangerous as the Sons, and the way he looked at her in this moment was definitely one of them.

Chapter Thirteen

He was tired, and he should sleep. Or eat. Or hydrate. He should do a long list of things that did not include sitting here wishing Liza would put her hands on more than just his battered face.

Her fingertips were solace against all the throbbing and burning. She was all he wanted, and he was tired enough of all *this* around them to think... It wouldn't be so wrong. It wouldn't compromise anything. Even knowing she thought his brother could have gone back. Even though *she'd* gone back.

Get up. Focus on the task at hand.

But he realized here, in this shimmering heat between him and Liza, that all the ways he'd been good and upstanding and dedicated to his job and the law the past fifteen years were only because she hadn't been there.

If she had been, everything would have come second to her. It always did. He leaned closer, keeping his arms at his sides even as her fingers slid through his hair.

"What are we doing here?" she asked, a whisper.

Her eyes were shiny, and she shook her head almost imperceptibly.

But she didn't move away. She didn't look away.

He knew what she was asking, but he didn't want to answer that question. "Waiting for the sun to set."

She tried to smile. "Well, if we're just waiting." She slid onto his lap, an easy, fluid movement that reminded him of a past that had been easier, oddly. He'd felt more in danger, more desperate back then, but it had been…youth. He'd thought he could fight for right and always win, but the past fifteen years had taught him otherwise at every turn.

Right didn't always win. Good didn't always come out on top. Yet he'd never been able to give up the hope that it would, that it could.

And here she was—his good, his hope. He gave himself leave to slide his hands down her back. Fifteen years since he'd touched her like this, but there was no difference in this moment.

"Do you remember our first time?" she asked, her hands cupping his jaw gently so as to not put too much pressure on his bruises, her mouth brushing just below his ear.

It was a visceral memory. An awful lot like this— his grandmother's barn instead of an abandoned shack, safety instead of danger, but Liza making all the moves and him accepting them, even as his rational mind told him not to. Too many things piling against him—knowing it wasn't the right time, that it wasn't right, and giving in anyway.

Because Liza was always *right*.

"Yeah, I remember."

"You wanted to wait. You always wanted to wait." She looked at him, so close they were nose to nose and he could count every faint freckle that dusted across her nose. He could catalog the way her face had changed and hadn't. But he only drowned in the dark brown of her eyes.

"What were you waiting for, Jamison?"

"I'm not sure I remember," he lied easily. Because lying to her about how he felt had always been the only thing that kept him on that path to good and right he'd always been striving for.

She didn't even pretend to consider his lie. "Of course you do. You remember everything."

His mouth quirked in spite of himself. He wasn't so sure he remembered everything, but he remembered enough. Things he didn't want to remember or rehash. So, he let his hands span her hips, pull her closer and more flush against him, where he ached for her.

Always her.

"I remember you."

She let out a shaky breath, searching his gaze for something. Something he didn't want to give, but she'd always found anyway—always would.

Always pulsed between them.

"What was it?" she asked, her voice still just a whisper, even if there was more urgency behind it. "Because I never understood. Maybe I was afraid to. I want to understand now. I know you wanted me,

I know you *loved* me, but you were always pushing me away. You didn't want to."

"No, I didn't want to." He could remember his own pious duty so well, and it hurt. It hurt because he didn't have it in him anymore. He was going to give in to this, and her, when he never would have before. Too old for pious duty, he supposed, or maybe just too cognizant of how little joy there was to be found when she wasn't with him.

"So, what was it, Jamison?"

She was sitting on his lap, the softest part of her nestled against the hardest part of him. Her hands held his face with a gentleness he'd never known in his life, and doubted she'd known in hers. His brother was out there. Her sister was missing. People were dead.

And they were rehashing old history while they waited for the sun to fall.

Somehow it seemed like all that fate he didn't believe in. Like they'd come to the moment made for rehashing. Rediscovering. Here, before they faced potential death and failure. Here, before the true war started—because this would be a war. With the Sons. With his father and hers.

So, he told her a truth he'd sworn he'd never tell her. "I wanted to do it right."

Her eyebrows drew together. "Right?"

"Get married. Be normal, upstanding people. You were too young for all that. So, I tried to wait until you weren't."

She sighed as if she was in some kind of pain.

Then she kissed him, slow and sweet, which was new enough. "I was never too young. And we're too old for all that now," she whispered against his mouth.

"Are we?"

Her body froze—except for her eyes—which whipped to his.

No matter how much of the past was here between them, he wasn't the same man he'd been. Because he hadn't been a *man*. Not really. He'd been filled with a youthful sense of right and wrong. An idea he could be *noble* and good. That life was black-and-white, and he would always follow the white.

But life was gray, pretty much always, for good men. Only men with empty souls could follow extremes to the ends of the earth.

So, this wouldn't be Liza pushing through his defenses. It wouldn't be her convincing him.

No, it would be him choosing. Finally, fully accepting the gray areas life threw at him. Because loving her had always been a little bit good *and* bad—as had she been herself. And was. And always would be.

Always. Always.

Slowly, watching her the whole time, he lifted her shirt up and over her head, revealing skin the sun almost never touched. Pale, pale white. A contrast to all that dark hair that swirled around her.

She'd always been a contrast. Dark and light. Right and wrong. Hope and fear. Instead of choosing one and fearing the other. He chose both, would love both.

The gold locket he'd given her once upon a time

hung from a chain. And while his brain told him not to, his heart was leading. When it came to her, it always had.

He reached out and flipped the locket open.

It had been a group shot, he remembered. Grandma had taken it with her old Polaroid camera—all the Wyatt boys, all the Knight girls in front of the barn. She'd taken a few because Brady kept accidentally blinking at the wrong moment.

Jamison had taken one of those and cut just him and Liza out, tucked it into the locket.

He opened the flimsy fake gold. Inside was the picture he'd cut out himself, put in there himself. A romantic gesture because he'd been trying to prove to her that life outside the Sons could be something *right*. Normal.

It shouldn't be that it still mattered, that somehow even knowing all he knew he wanted to find a way to give her that. It shouldn't be that fifteen years felt like nothing since the moment he'd caught her trying to break into his office.

But it was.

He moved her onto her back, underneath him. He touched her, a choice—not only giving in. He kissed her—mouth, neck, shoulder. He touched her, gently and reverently. She pulled off his shirt, touching him until his skin felt like it was too tight, and only she could take away all the pressure building inside him.

Because only she could.

He slid off her pants, careful of her leg injury. She

tugged at his, until they were both naked for each other. Joined. Like they'd always been meant to be.

The ache was unbearable and he wanted to live in it forever as she arched against him, as she whispered his name, begging for that unnamed release.

Then slow and sweet was gone. That old desperation conjured by talk of the past...by talk of a future.

Knowing history couldn't be erased, and the future wasn't a given, they gave themselves to each other. Falling over a blissful edge wrapped up together, just like then. Just like now.

"Liza."

Liza didn't want to leave this warm bubble of sleep, no matter how incessant Jamison's voice was. She wasn't sleeping on the floor, and she wasn't cold. It was nice here, and she burrowed deeper into the soft blanket under her cheek.

"Liza."

But she was colder than she had been, because Jamison's body was no longer next to her. She blinked her eyes open. There was still a hint of sun shining through the window, so they couldn't have slept more than an hour or two.

She glared at him. Then remembered the whole point of her life was saving her sister, not sleeping.

Certainly not having sex with her ex-boyfriend from fifteen years ago.

But looking at that serious expression, the mussed hair and bruised face, she thought *ex-boyfriend* was hardly the right word. He was the love of her life. Then. Now. Always.

She'd said they were too old for things like marriage and being normal and doing it right, and he'd said "Are we?" like they had some kind of future spreading out before them.

It would be suicide to believe there was, but she could see it too clearly, feel it too clearly to resist.

If she survived this, maybe they could find each other again. Maybe.

But just like always, they had to survive first.

"I found something," he said, his voice devoid of all emotion. His eyes, though... She could see he felt everything she did right there in his eyes.

But he'd found something. "What kind of something?" she asked in a sigh.

"Get dressed."

She grumbled through it, finding her clothes had been laid out neatly beside her. She almost asked him where he came from—but she knew his kindness was simply a mix of two things. One, the fact that he'd spent his first five years living with Grandma Pauline and his mother, before his mother had been fully converted to the Sons' way of life and Ace had decided he didn't want any good influence on his children. Two, something innate inside him.

Dressed, she pushed herself off the bed. "It's still light out."

"Not for long, but that's not why I woke you up." He nodded toward the hall and led her back to the bathroom.

"I got up to use the bathroom and I saw this weird light. Green. Coming from a crack in the wall. I guess it was too light to notice it earlier."

"Let me guess. Nuclear waste."

But he didn't even try to crack a smile at her joke. He squatted down next to a place where he'd apparently pulled off a piece of the wall. Inside the dark hole was something completely incongruous to this whole place. Some kind of...computer.

"What does it mean?" she asked. There were boxes and flashing circles on the screen. The green light Jamison must have seen was from the power light on the side of the laptop.

"Well, whoever was here before us left this behind. It means we're not safe here. That's for darn sure, but... It's explosives, Liza. Whatever this is, it's controlling explosives."

"What?" she all but screeched, trying to figure out why on earth he was being so calm about being blown up.

"I don't understand it all—don't know enough about it. But it's marking down time before explosives go off."

"Here?"

"No. No, I think..." He shook his head. "I don't know enough about it, but it might be your father's place. This is something like a blueprint," he said, pointing to the screen. "There's a house—decent sized. A horse stable here. A shed of some kind over here." He traced the squares and rectangles on the screen. "And each of these blinking dots is a point where explosives will go off. Is my guess anyway."

She grabbed his arm, suddenly icy cold. "But Gigi is there."

"We don't know that for sure," he said, so measured and so *cop* she wanted to scream.

"But she could be, Jamison. She *could* be there, and someone's going to blow it up." She squeezed the arm she was holding. "Cody. Cody wasn't that far away. He's the only one we saw, and if this is blowing up the Sons, this has to be Cody's. They're not blowing up themselves."

"I wouldn't put it past them, but…" He sighed. "Cody seems likely."

"Get him to stop it. Jamison—you have to get him to stop it."

"How? I don't know where he went. He told me to stay away."

Liza whirled out of the bathroom. She didn't have time to argue with him. She didn't have time for anything.

"We have to split up. I've got try to find the house and rescue Gigi. You find Cody." She grabbed her boots, and he grabbed her wrist, stopping her forward movement.

"We don't split up. *You* said that."

She didn't want to; that was the worst part. "We do when a little girl's life is at stake," she returned, jerking her arm out of his grasp. "There's not enough time to do both together. Someone needs to stop Cody, and someone needs to get Gigi. Now."

"We don't know where that house is. We don't know where Cody is. We don't, in fact, know where Gigi is."

"But we know they're not here."

He raked a hand through his hair. "I'm not suggesting we stay here and do nothing. I'm suggesting we *think*."

"Think about what? There is no time to think. You have to go where we were and try to find Cody. I have to go toward where we think my father's place might be and get Gigi. We don't have time for anything else." She sat on the bed and quickly tied her boots.

"Are you going to fight off your father and any other Sons by yourself with one gun? And let's say you could—when you get Gigi, what are you going to do with her? You can't just go in there and *die*. That doesn't serve anyone."

She stood and looked him square in the eye. "I couldn't live with myself, if Gigi dies and I didn't even try to get to her in time. Jamison, look at me." She wasted precious seconds waiting until he did. "If it were one of your brothers when they were four and helpless, or even one of the Knight girls, what would you do? Put yourself in my shoes."

"I'm already in your shoes. You think Gigi being hurt would mean nothing to me?"

The fact that she knew it would mean nearly as much to him as it did to her, even though he'd never met Gigi, only made her heart hurt more. But she'd wasted too much time. She hadn't started on this journey to find Jamison again. Anything they'd shared in this cabin was only…a weakness. One she couldn't keep letting change her. "We don't have time. We do not have time. I have to go and so do you." She grabbed the gun, then swung her pack onto her back. She opened her mouth to tell him to move, but he spoke first.

"I love you—"

She should have known he'd fight dirty. But she wouldn't fall for it, even as her heart swelled and her eyes pricked with tears. "Jamison, don't try to use—"

"I have always loved you. I will always love you." He was calm. Dead serious.

And it couldn't—*didn't*—matter.

"All the love in the world doesn't matter if she dies and I didn't try to get to her. I'll die with her, one way or another."

"If you die, so does she. I want you to remember that. I had to. More than once did I have to remind myself that nothing good happened for my brothers if I was dead in a ditch. Find the house. Find Gigi. Do what you have to do to get her to safety—but you can't be reckless doing what you have to do. You can't risk yourself, because that only risks her. Do you understand me?"

She didn't, for a few seconds, because he was… He was letting her go. Not that she would have let him stop her, but she thought he'd try. She'd thought he'd…

It didn't matter. Because he was letting her go without further argument or impediment. She moved onto her toes and pressed her mouth to his—hard and fast.

Then she gave him what he'd given her. "I love you. I have always loved you. I will always love you—whatever happens."

"As soon as I get Cody to stop this, I'll be there. If you get her out—we'll meet back here. Understood?"

She nodded. He grabbed his own pack and handed her the walkie from it. "You keep this on. If they're in there, one of the channels should pick it up if they're sending messages outside."

"But you—"

"I won't be next to the house they're in. Presumably." He zipped up his pack and shouldered the larger burden. He reattached his holstered weapon around his waist.

She didn't want to take this next leg alone. She'd gotten so used to being alone she would have considered herself immune to feeling this again, to needing someone again.

Here it was, though, an ache of longing. She wanted someone's hand to hold. Someone to patch up her wounds and vice versa. She wanted his quiet strength and surety leading her into saving her sister.

Didn't she already know she couldn't do this alone? She'd failed Marci and Carlee and—

"Liza."

She looked up at him, panic an icy cold bucket of reality on all those plans she'd been brimming to fulfill.

"We're still together in this. We're just working

on two different ends of the same rope. We meet in the middle."

"I—"

"We'll meet in the middle. Now, here." He pulled his map, the marked one he'd spent *years* on, out of his pocket and handed it to her. "This might help. There are extra batteries for the headlamp in the bottom of your pack if you start to lose power. Okay?"

She stared at the map, then him. He was giving her a pep talk. Encouraging her. When she knew very well he did not want her to do it. When, if this was fifteen years ago, he already would have locked her in the cabin so he could do it all himself.

I wanted to do it right.

Letting her go, trusting her to get to Gigi like she trusted him to get to Cody and stop the explosives.

On a deep breath, she nodded. "We meet in the middle."

Then she walked out into the darkness, ready to do whatever it took to get Gigi to that middle.

Chapter Fourteen

With every step he took, Jamison cursed himself for letting Liza go alone. He should have gone with her. They could have liberated Gigi together and let every other part of the Sons compound burn.

But there were too many what-ifs. What if the explosives went off sooner rather than later? What if more than just Gigi was at stake when it came to innocent bystanders? There wasn't time. No matter how he tried to convince himself those were the reasons he'd let her go, it wasn't anything rational or reasonable.

He'd seen that look on Liza's face as she'd hesitated back there in the cabin. The way she'd been determined, and then doubt had crept in and left her frozen. She'd needed someone to trust her, to tell her she could do it.

Maybe she'd always needed that from him and he'd never seen it. Maybe that was what a lot of people in his life needed from him—not someone to sweep in and fix and save everything, but someone to say they could handle it on their own.

There was no use going through the past, no use thinking about all the ways he might have stifled his brothers, but he could fix his present.

Liza was a strong and capable woman, and she needed a win. She needed a few people to believe she could accomplish that win. Gigi needed to be alive. Jamison had to believe Liza when she said she couldn't survive losing another person, and he had to do everything in his power to help.

Which meant he had to stop the explosives. As quickly as possible, and at whatever cost. He had no experience with computers *or* explosives, so poking around on the computer was only a dangerous possibility.

He had to find Cody because Cody knew *all* about computers. Cody had gotten a degree in computer science—the only one of them to make it to college—not that they'd given him much of a choice. Once teachers had started commenting on Cody's intelligence in middle school, Jamison and his brothers had done everything in their power to learn about how to get their baby brother into college.

Cody had protested at first, made noise about the police academy, but eventually he'd given in to the pressure and gone off to South Dakota State. It wasn't Harvard, but it was something.

And Cody had used those opportunities. He'd done internships within the CIA. He'd finished his degree with honors. For the past few years he'd spoken of an on-again, off-again freelance computer job that kept him in Wyoming. He only came home around Christmas and never gave much by way of details.

If they weren't Cody's explosives, Cody would at least have a better idea of what was going on. Jamison had to believe Cody was involved with whatever was happening. There was no other explanation for him roaming around the Black Hills, carrying what appeared to be a Sons walkie and communicating in Morse code, all very far from where he was supposed to be.

Jamison reached the spot where he'd originally run into Cody. He worried less about his headlamp now, because while the threat of being caught still existed, it was a risk he'd have to take if he was going to find Cody.

Jamison stopped and looked around. He'd been thinking about Liza and his brother, but he hadn't been thinking strategically. Cody had been striding away from the clearing—opposite to the cabin. Jamison thought about the map, about where they thought Liza's father's cabin was.

Immediately, he turned west. If his instincts were right, and he had the map clear in his head, Cody had been going in the direction of Tony Dean's place. Maybe to lay the explosives? Or something else to do with them?

There was only one way to find out.

Jamison didn't take the same path Liza had taken. They'd have better luck finding the place if they weren't approaching it from the same angle. So, he thought about the direction he'd seen Cody go.

Every so many steps he made an adjustment to the map in his head. Turning, thinking, analyzing.

He heard a crack. The whisper of movement. Slowly, cautiously, he moved one hand to his gun and the other hand to the switch of his headlamp. Another whisper, this time on the opposite side of him.

He switched off the light, plunging him and whoever—or whatever—else into darkness, and took a leap away from the spot he'd been standing in.

But that crashed him into something—and since he hadn't been standing that close to any trees, it had to be a person.

So, Jamison fought. Trying to wrestle the other person underneath him. The other man pushed but didn't hit, then whispered viciously.

"Stop trying to hit me, you moron," Cody's voice hissed.

Jamison stilled, then untangled himself from his brother and got to his feet. "You didn't think to say, 'Hey, Jamison, I'm lurking around the woods you're hiking through.' Who's the moron? Thinking I won't fight?"

"Shut up for a second, and don't turn on that idiotic light," Cody growled.

Jamison listened, though he didn't particularly want to take orders from his baby brother. After a few seconds, Cody made an irritated noise. "What are you doing?"

"Are we speaking now? Or did you want to hold hands and tap each other more?"

"Now's not the time for your sad attempts at humor. You can't go that direction, Jamison. Go back the way you came. Stop trying to do…whatever it is you're trying to do."

"I can't do that."

"This isn't a joke, and it's no place for—no offense—a sleepy small town's sheriff's deputy. I don't know what you think you're up to with Liza Dean of all people, but I don't have time. You have to vacate the premises. Both of you."

"If I could do that, Cody, I would have done it the first time you asked. I'm not here as a sheriff, and Liza isn't here as… Never mind. Listen to me. Are you the one with the explosives?"

Cody shoved him. Hard. Jamison scowled, though it was lost in the dark.

"Are you trying to get us all killed?" Cody hissed.

"I don't think you understand. If this is you, you can't do it. You can't… There are innocent lives at stake."

"There are Sons' lives at stake," Cody said with a cold fierceness that had Jamison feeling a chill go right through him. "I don't care much about those," Cody added.

"What about the kids?"

"Kids? There aren't kids there. Do you think I don't know what I'm doing? That I'm some rogue idiot trying to blow someone up for fun? For revenge. I have been canvassing this area and that house. I…I can't get into this with you. I know you fancy yourself savior supreme along with big brother, but this is bigger than you, Jamison. Get Liza and go and leave me to it."

"What about Carlee Bright?"

This time Cody didn't shove him. He grabbed him by the shirtfront. "You have no idea—no idea—what you are getting involved in."

And because his brother seemed genuinely—*scared* wasn't the right word—affected, concerned, sharp and poised, like a blade, Jamison didn't fight him off. He let Cody have his grip as he spoke calmly and quietly.

"No. I don't. But I know that Liza's sister saw Carlee murdered, and then Gigi disappeared after telling Liza. I know Tony killed Carlee—or at least was there when it happened. I know, having done no canvassing and spending no time here, that Gigi is four years old and in exactly the kind of danger we can imagine."

"Tony comes and goes. Three of his henchmen. A few women are in there always, but no kids."

"Did you check the shack? The stables?"

"I've been watching. There isn't—"

"What have you been watching, Cody? Not everything. Not every inch. You've been watching Tony and his men, but have you been paying attention?"

"You don't know what you're getting yourself mixed up in, Jamison. Go home. Go back to Bonesteel. Let me take care of this."

"I can't."

"Right. You can't. You can't listen to me, and you can't trust me. But you trust Liza. Who went back."

"I trust Liza, who's trying to save someone she loves. I know something about that. You have to stop the explosives, Cody. You *have to*. Until we know for sure."

"It's not my call, Jamison."

Jamison put his hand over Cody's, still twisted in his shirt. Not to pull it off, but to get through to his brother. "Make it your call. Now."

Cody's grip stayed tight on Jamison's shirt. "You don't get to boss me around anymore, big brother."

But someone apparently did. "What on earth are you involved in?"

"Bigger things than saving one little girl."

"There's no bigger thing than trying to save the kids caught in that place. If it was as easy as blowing up all the bad men, we could have done that twenty years ago. It isn't so easy, Cody. I know you know that. Somewhere deep down you have to know that."

Cody released Jamison's shirt, giving him another slight shove as he did. Then he swore, viciously, in the dark.

Jamison waited, though every second that ticked by tested his patience and his worry over Liza. Cody was doing something, tapping at what sounded like computer keys, but there was no light, no sign of what he was doing.

After a few minutes he took Jamison's hand and pressed a small rectangle into it.

"You're going to go to the compound." Cody

swore at himself as if he already regretted giving that order. "You're going to search the stables—there is nothing going on in the shack or the house. The stables… It's just horses, but my men did the search. Not me. It wasn't my assignment, but…"

"Assignment?"

"You'll search the stables—that's it. If it's clear— you press that button twice and you get the hell out because I'm blowing the place up. If, on the insanely off chance my guys missed something and there are innocent people on the premises, you press it once and only once."

"And if they're there—then what?"

"Then, I might be able to get you some help. *Might.* But not before I've got proof, maybe not even if I do."

"Cody—"

"No questions. You can't worry about me, brother. You've got bigger things to worry about right now."

Jamison hated that it was true. "You'll stay safe."

"Safe? What do you take me for, Jamison? Certainly not a Wyatt," Cody said with just the tiniest hint of humor. "Now go. And hurry."

That was just what Jamison did.

LIZA NEARLY TRIPPED over the first sign she was on the right track. The metal glinted in the light of the moon—which had been bright enough for her to keep the headlamp off. Occasionally she'd use the beam to check the map, but otherwise it made her feel too conspicuous.

Now she flipped it on and found a little pink tricycle, covered in dirt and pine needles like it hadn't been used in a while. Based on the fact it was early spring, it probably hadn't been.

She tried not to get her hopes up. A little pink tricycle could mean anything. But mostly it meant a little girl had been around here somewhere at some point, and a little girl was what she was looking for.

She turned the headlamp off and looked up. Off in the distance, she thought she saw the hint of lights. Lights.

Slowly, carefully, she moved toward it. The closer she got, the more the trees crowded together—providing excellent cover. But after walking awhile, she nearly sobbed in relief, because through the trees she saw the warm glow of lights dancing in windows. *Windows.*

In the moonlight and starlight, the shadow of a big, beautiful cabin loomed. It had to be what she was looking for. It *had* to be.

Knowing her father, she was sure there would be all sorts of security. Men watching from all angles. Cameras, maybe. Anything was possible because this whole place was very unlike the Sons. They liked their tents and shacks and things you could leave behind, and quickly. They preferred caves for big meetings and "justice" being served because evidence wouldn't be found.

This whole spread before her was very strange—and spoke to a permanence the Sons had never attempted before.

Maybe, just maybe, it could be their downfall.

But that wasn't the point of right now. Now she was solely focused on finding Gigi. She stood behind a tree, forcing herself to slow her breathing, to think rationally.

She'd made it, found her father's place. Now she just had to find Gigi. And avoid all detection by the Sons, and hope Jamison found Cody to stop the explosives.

She knew she should entertain the thought Jamison could fail, but it wasn't possible. *Jamison* and *failure* in the same sentence didn't make sense. She couldn't get her brain or her heart to think it possible.

It didn't matter—because she had a job to do here. A girl to find and protect. And if someone found her or them, she had a gun. She'd defend herself and Gigi.

Yes, a *gun will defend you from a horde of gang members*. Why did she think she could do this?

Because it's the only choice.

The only choice. She repeated that to herself as she turned back to face the house. She searched the dark, seeing a dozen shadows that looked like they were moving toward her.

Her imagination and tricks of the moonlight. She listened to the night. No footsteps. Just the wind and the trees and…

Horses. The distinct sound of a horse snuffling. She must be close to the stables, and Gigi had mentioned a horse. Maybe that would give her some kind of clue, or at least a better, safer vantage point.

Liza moved toward the noise and realized she

was ridiculously close to a large, squat building that clearly housed the stables. She reached out and touched the wood. She was at the back, maybe, because there was no door or window on this side.

She used her hands to guide her as she felt her way toward the front. The door into the building had a big chain and padlock on it. Strange.

Dread crept along Liza's spine, but she inched forward, still trying to find the source of the horse noises.

Eventually she came to a high window, the soft nose of a horse sticking out of it. There was something like a door—also locked with a padlock—but the door itself was more like a gate—big bars with space between them.

Liza crouched down and looked through the gate, seeing if she could peer into the stables for any clues. She was too close to the house to turn her headlamp on, so she had to hope moonlight was enough as she squinted into the dark.

At first, it was just moving, melting dark that she couldn't be sure was *actually* moving, or just her eyes playing tricks. But as she watched and her eyes adjusted, she was almost certain she saw something moving around deep in the stables. It could be anything. Other animals. Mice.

She shuddered, squinting through the gate until she was almost certain she saw…

Eyes.

Liza kept perfectly still, watching as the eyes moved

back into the shadows. But something was moving closer. She held her breath, adjusted the gun in her grip.

The figure was small. Too small to be a man. Too small to be anything but a child.

"Gigi," Liza whispered, more hope than certainty.

"Sissy?"

Liza nearly collapsed. She swallowed down tears as pudgy fingers curled around the gate, Gigi's dirty face peering at her through the spaces in the bars.

"I'm not supposed to be here," Gigi whispered, glancing warily at the cabin.

Liza tried not to sob as she fell to her knees to put her eye level with Gigi. "I'm not either, baby."

"I want Mommy."

"I know. I know." Liza studied the gate. The height from the ground to the top of the window. "Can you climb up here?"

Gigi looked up, then her mouth curved just a hint. "George will help me."

George? "No—no, don't tell any—"

But Gigi was scurrying away. Liza let out a sigh of relief when she only went over to the horse in the stall.

"Mommy taught me a trick," Gigi said—too loud, far too loud.

Liza pressed her face to the gate. "You've got to whisper, baby. We have to be careful. Anyone could be out here and the only way we get out of here safe is if we're very, very quiet."

"No. It's meeting time. We're all alone until the

lights upstairs go out. Then someone comes with supper."

"They're keeping you out here?" Even though all signs pointed to it, she could hardly believe it. Tony Dean was a monster, and she'd been locked in her share of rooms and closets, growing up with him as a father. But Gigi was so sweet.

Silly to think there was any difference between how Tony would have treated her, and how he would have treated Gigi. Daughters were useless, until they weren't. Why wouldn't he treat Gigi just as badly, if not worse?

Gigi didn't respond to Liza's question out loud. It was possible she nodded or shook her head, but it was too hard to see in the dark. Gigi whispered something to the animal, then it seemed to... It seemed to kneel.

Liza fairly gasped as Gigi shimmied up the horse's large body into a sitting position on the horse's back. Liza heard a thud and realized that Gigi was giving the horse a pat as it got back onto its feet. Higher up, the moonlight glinted against Gigi's blond hair and big smile. Her grip was in the horse's mane, and she learned forward and pressed her cheek to the horse.

"Mommy said George would help me escape someday," Gigi said, sadness creeping into her tone.

"Your mommy was right," Liza managed to squeak, ignoring the tears tracking down her cheeks. "Come here, George," she encouraged the horse.

The massive horse made its way close enough to the gate so Liza could hold out her arms. Gigi pulled herself onto the top of the gate without hesitation, like she'd done this before. Who knew, maybe she had. Maybe she and Carlee had worked on this very escape.

Liza couldn't think about that too much right now. She held out her arms and Gigi jumped into them with an easy trust that made tears clog her throat.

Liza hugged Gigi tight, wanting to cry over the little girl being in her arms again, but there was no time. Liza glanced at the upstairs lights—still on— but that didn't mean no one was watching.

"Daddy said he's going to kill George. When the time is right," Gigi said, laying her cheek against Liza's shoulders and squeezing tight as if to assure herself Liza was real.

Liza didn't know what to say to that. This horse had potentially saved Gigi's life in this moment. "No, we won't let that happen." Somehow, they'd figure out a way to come back and get George.

Now, it was up to Liza to save Gigi. She was here, impossibly here, with Gigi in her arms. Everything was going to be okay.

Gigi being out here by herself was some miracle and Liza had to use that miracle to her advantage. "Listen, baby. We're going to run away, okay. You just hold on to me and be real quiet."

Gigi lifted her head. "What about the others?"

Liza's blood went cold. "What others?"

Gigi pointed back at the stables. "The others. I'm supposed to stay with the others."

Hell.

Chapter Fifteen

Jamison was starting to believe he'd headed in the wrong direction. It was dark and he was tired and maybe he'd lost all sense of direction. Maybe he was walking in circles, destined to cause everyone in his life to die.

He shoved that thought away. Luckily, he had some practice with battling those voices, those doubts. He hadn't let anyone die when he'd been a kid. Under no circumstances would he allow it to happen now.

So, he kept moving forward and didn't allow doubts to threaten. Second-guessing himself *would* get him lost and likely get someone killed. He had to believe in himself, in his abilities. Like he was believing in Cody to do the right thing, and Liza to take care of herself.

Living life or death so often meant constantly *believing* in people. He knew some cops who got too bitter, or too arrogant, who didn't think anyone could ever have their back.

But it was a death sentence when you knew life

was on the line. Hope was so often the real difference between life and death.

Not just his or Liza's or Gigi's, but Cody's, too, now.

His brother was involved in *something*, God only knew what. Considering there were explosives involved, Jamison had a hard time believing it was something within the law. That ate at him, if he'd let it.

And if he let it, he wasn't worrying over walking in the wrong direction.

Hadn't Jamison and his other brothers worked their butts off to give Cody every opportunity away from the Sons? Instead, he was in the thick of things—plotting with *other people* to blow things up.

It just about figured.

He might have let that guilt and irritation fuel his forward progress, but he came up short when he saw lights ahead. The kind of light that came from homes. Warm and glowing dots in the distance.

Homes. It was so weird to think of the Sons in association with a *home*. Cabin, shack, stables. Sure, they'd probably stolen it from someone they'd killed, but it was so unlike the Sons' MO Jamison had grown up with. He had to wonder how well he knew how to fight this new version of his father's gang.

One that put down roots, and potentially sold and traded people. Liza had told him it had changed and in a way he'd understood that power and violence had grown unchecked. He'd understood he needed to look at them differently, maybe even fight them differently, but this new development of them doing "*normal* people" things while also potentially trafficking little girls… It seriously messed with him if he thought too much about it.

So, he couldn't. He had to focus on how to fight it, because whether he was good at it now or not didn't matter. He was still doing it.

He crept closer and closer to the light, pausing every so often to listen. Mostly it was all wind and branches rustling, but the closer he got, the more he thought he heard…whispering.

He moved toward the noise, continuing to pause, trying to determine if the voices were male or female. The Sons only used men for security or outside watches, and they wouldn't necessarily have cause to whisper.

Jamison had to believe it wasn't armed Sons men talking, but he couldn't see the figures yet to tell for sure, so he could only creep closer and closer until the moonlight gave him some clues.

There was a small figure crouched next to a big building, and a larger figure trying to scale a…gate of some kind. Like they were trying to get inside— like *she* was trying to get inside.

"Liza."

The figure bobbled, then fell to the ground, though landing on her feet. "Hurry," she strained to whisper.

He moved toward them both, noticing the way the

little girl scurried behind Liza's legs and held on to them for dear life.

"Gigi, it's okay," Liza soothed, putting her hand on the girl's head. "This is Jamison. He's my friend and he's going to help us. I promise."

The little girl vigorously shook her head.

Liza crouched next to the girl as Jamison came closer. "Jamison is one of the few very good guys around. He saved me once. A long time ago. I promise he's one of the good guys. He's going to help."

"You found her," Jamison said stupidly. He couldn't believe it. Here they both stood, alive and well. Now all they had to do was—

"She says there are more inside the stables. More girls," Liza's voice cracked on the last word.

So much for things being easy. Jamison let out a breath. "I found Cody. I just have to get a message to him and we'll stop the explosives." With nerveless fingers, Jamison pulled the device Cody had given him and hit the button once. It solved one problem, but not the other just as deadly threatening problem. "That should give us time. But we still have to get out of here. All we've managed to fix is the explosives situation."

"Take Gigi. I'll get the other girls."

Jamison didn't even pretend to consider that. He strode for the gate and studied it in the moonlight. "Give me a boost. I'll go over and get them and hand them off to you. I'll be able to get back out easier than you will, especially with your leg, and Gigi will feel safer with you out here."

"Jamison."

"No time to waste." He adjusted his pack and put his hands atop the stall door. There'd be no way or time to get that padlock off, but he wasn't altogether certain he could boost himself back over. Still, better him stuck in here than her.

He pulled himself up onto the ledge. He couldn't get all the way up—it was just a pinch too high—so he instructed Liza to push him the rest of the way over.

He fell, and in the dark he couldn't make it a particularly graceful fall. He landed on his side, jarring his elbow and his hip against the solid dirt ground that smelled like manure. His body vibrated with pain, but nothing was broken—yet.

Unfortunately the thudding, clumsy fall sent the horse into a bit of a panic. It whinnied and reared. Jamison was far more worried about the noise than any potential bodily harm. Nonetheless, he scurried back onto his feet trying to calm the horse.

"Shh. Shh. It's all right," he muttered, holding up his hands. The horse pranced in the small space of its outdoor stall, kicking up smells and noises and the potential for them all to die. "Shh," Jamison continued, stepping a little closer. The horse continued to move nervously, but Jamison managed to get close enough to touch, to reassure.

He gently smoothed a hand over the horse's flank and it settled some. It was likely somewhat used to strange men coming and going. After a few more calming words and soothing pets, the horse calmed completely.

He glanced back at the gate, Liza and Gigi standing there watching him. A lot riding on him and no time to waste.

With the horse stilled, he moved past it and into the dark of the stable building. He hesitated, looking around, but he couldn't even see if there were windows or more gates. He'd need a light, as much as that was dangerous. He couldn't do it without one.

He took the headlamp off his head and held it pointed to the ground as he flipped it on. By keeping the beam pointed downward, he hoped to avoid detection from the outside. Dirty hay was under his feet as he slowly swept the beam around. He found himself in a bigger stall. There was a door, and it was luckily unlatched. Presumably it was how Gigi had gotten into the stall, and to Liza, in the first place.

He slid through the stall door opening and into a long cement hallway of sorts. Around him were all sorts of stalls. He didn't hear anyone or anything, which led him to believe they only had one horse.

And room for plenty of other horrors. The silence was what really got to him. There should be shuffling or moving, breathing or whispering if there were more people back here.

But he was a cop, and he knew his duty. He began to search the stable building like he would any other. He took each room methodically, carefully, keeping his beam of light low and away from anything that looked like a window to the outside. He checked corners and behind doors in every stall.

He doubted Gigi had made up the story about more people being in here, but maybe she was confused. Maybe they were somewhere else. But Gigi had somehow gotten to Liza, and even at four it wouldn't be that confusing to know she'd left a group of people.

Why would Gigi have permission to get out to the horse, though? Special favors for the boss's daughter? Doubtful if she'd witnessed her father murder her mother.

Jamison swept through another stall. He had yet to find a door that was padlocked shut like the outside doors, but he supposed locking the doors to escape from the outside was protection enough.

There was only one room left. It wasn't like the stalls—it had a full door and was toward the back. Like some kind of stable hand's quarters or a manager's office. Jamison crept closer and still heard nothing that give any inclination human beings were trapped inside.

Living human beings anyway. It was possible Gigi had been left with dead bodies. He wouldn't put it past the sons, and if they'd killed Carlee over this, who else might they have?

Still, though his soul recoiled from having to face it, the potential for dead bodies was one he'd live with, because he knew how to deal with horrors. He'd been dealing his whole life.

He would do whatever it took to protect the

innocent—he'd made that promise to himself and the world a long time ago.

As he eased open the door and swept his light into the last room, he nearly sagged with relief. For the first time he found something besides empty cement or dirty hay. At least ten girls were huddled in the corner. They winced against the light, holding on to each other and pushing closer together as if they could become invisible if they only pressed together tightly enough.

They had it down to an art form. He hadn't heard them until he'd stepped inside. They'd made themselves so still, so silent, Jamison hadn't heard *ten* girls until he'd been standing practically next to them.

Jamison had to access the cop part of himself that compartmentalized the cold horror away and act.

"I'm not here to hurt you," he said quietly, keeping exactly where he was in the entrance to the stall so they didn't feel threatened. He turned the light to shine on him, rather than them. "I'm not with the Sons. We're going to get you out of here, but you're going to have to listen to me, and you're going to have to be very quiet."

They huddled closer, and he doubted they believed him, but he couldn't exactly force them out, either.

"I'm a police officer. Here…" It took precious time they didn't have, but he couldn't drag these girls out kicking and screaming. Not just because they'd be caught, but because these girls had been through enough.

He shrugged off his pack and unzipped the small, interior pocket. He grabbed the badge he'd shoved into the pack what felt like a million years ago but was only a few days. "Here's my badge." He shone the light on it. "I'm a police officer. I'm going to help you."

Of course, if they were all Sons girls they'd been taught at a young age to distrust police, but he had to hope in this current situation they might change their mind.

No one moved. No one spoke. He returned the badge to its pocket, reshouldered his pack and put the lamp on his head.

"I just need you to come with me. One at a time. I'm going to take you to the horse's stable outside. I'm going to help you over the gate. There's a woman and the little girl who was in here with you waiting. Gigi? She's already out. Once we're all out, we're going to run."

"They'll kill us if we run," one of the girls whispered.

"Not if I can help it." Jamison knew enough about getting people out of a dark situation that flat out lying didn't often produce the desired results. But neither did he want to give the unvarnished truth to a bunch of scared *girls*. The oldest couldn't be more than twelve, at best. Disgust and horror clogged his throat, but he had to speak.

Put it away. Focus on getting them out.

"They have to catch us first. Would you rather stay here or would you rather try to survive?"

There was nothing but silence. Still, Jamison

wouldn't give up. Not until they were all out. "One at a time. Who wants to be first?"

He waited. Too long. Too damn long. But finally one of the girls struggled onto her feet. A few of the other girls told her to stop, but she shook her head. She was one of the older ones.

"I'd rather die than stay here," she said firmly.

Jamison nodded. He wanted to offer a hand, but he figured that would be more threatening. "You just follow me out, okay?"

She nodded, and as he walked back the way he'd come, she followed. He turned off his light as he reached the outdoor part of the stable, then moved forward.

When the girl saw Liza and Gigi, she ran toward the gate and fell to her knees with a sob. "It's true," she whispered. "You're going to save us."

"We're going to try," Liza said, patting the girl's hand that was clutching the bars of the gate. "Let Jamison lift you over. Then I'll catch you."

She nodded, looking back at Jamison. He and Liza worked together to get her over the gate, and she immediately started to cry in earnest.

"It has to be quicker than this," Liza whispered to Jamison as Gigi wrapped her arms around the crying girl.

"I know" was all he said, before he went back in, hoping the next girls would follow.

LIZA WATCHED THE house between each girl Jamison brought out. This was taking too long. The upstairs lights couldn't stay on forever. Eventually someone would be coming with the girls' supper, according to Gigi.

And Gigi wouldn't leave her side.

Liza had instructed the eight girls Jamison had gotten out so far to go hide in the woods. One girl knew a spot where she thought they could all be un-detected if the main house flipped on the floodlights. But Liza hadn't been able to get Gigi to go with them, and she'd started to throw a fit when one of the girls had tried to carry her away.

She was in too much danger here, but Liza didn't know what else to do. The girls coming out of the stables had been hurt. So much worse was waiting for them if she and Jamison left them here.

There was only now to save them. Save them they would. Things were going better than Liza could have expected and the lights upstairs were still on. Every second that clicked by, Liza's heart beat harder against her ribs.

Maybe they'd make it. Maybe they'd get every girl out before those lights clicked off. Maybe—

The upstairs went suddenly black. Liza almost couldn't believe her eyes as the entire top story of the cabin in the distance went dark. She froze for a second or two, but Gigi's voice brought her back from that icy precipice of panic.

"The lights went out, sissy," Gigi whispered, fear emanating from every word. "They're coming."

"I know, baby. I know," Liza said. She had to do something. She had to act.

But Jamison said there were two more girls. The lights had gone out, which meant someone was coming. If they were found…

Finally, Jamison appeared with another girl.

"The lights went out, Jamison. They're coming."

"But Jenni is still in there," the little girl he was leading whimpered. She didn't look much older than Gigi. Jamison had to lift her up and practically set her on top of the gate. Liza pulled her down.

"Come over yourself," Liza said to Jamison, trying not to sound as panicked as she felt, for the girls' sake. "Take the girls somewhere safe. I'll get the last one."

"No. Not enough time. Besides, they'll all be more comfortable running with a woman. You start moving. The last one's a little afraid, but her sister here was very brave. She'll follow me now, so we'll meet you. Head for the cabin. Hopefully Cody is there."

Liza didn't want to leave this spot—for that last girl too afraid to leave, for Jamison too brave and good to leave a scared little girl. But the more people were here, the less chance they had of escape. All of them.

"Come on, girls," she said, taking the two little hands in hers. It just about killed her, but she started walking toward where the other girls had gone. She'd get them and start heading for the cabin.

She wouldn't look back, didn't have time to.

If Jamison didn't follow, she'd drop the girls with Cody and go get him. She wouldn't let him sacrifice himself for…

Wouldn't she do the same?

Shouldn't you do the same?

She looked down at Gigi, who hadn't left her side. No. Like Jamison had said back at the original cabin, if she died, the likelihood Gigi did, too, increased. Gigi was the priority. Until she was safe, nothing else mattered.

She couldn't think about saving Jamison just yet. So, she just had to believe he'd save the last girl *and* himself. Of course he would. Jamison always did.

She urged the girls with her to run, though they both hesitated with the dark around them. Liza heard a door creak open, then slam closed somewhere far off.

Someone was coming.

"Come on. We have to hurry." She wished she could pick them both up, but that wouldn't help any.

She walked, trying to hurry, holding them up when the girls stumbled and keeping their movement forward no matter what. They were doing all right, making fair progress by Liza's estimation when her foot got caught on something and she pitched forward, the girls tumbling with her.

Liza didn't cry out, though falling hurt like hell. Though she was pretty sure she'd twisted her ankle or broken all of her stitches or both. But it didn't matter. Liza struggled to her feet, pulling Gigi and the other girl to theirs, as well.

They were both crying, quietly at first, but the pitch and volume began to increase. Growing louder and louder in the silent woods.

"Hush, now. We don't want anyone to hear us."

She knelt and squeezed both girls to her sides, pressing kisses to their temples. "I know it's hard, but we have to do this hard thing to be safe. What's your name, sweetheart?"

The little girl sniffled. "Bette."

"Okay, Bette. I'm going to carry you for a bit. Then it'll be Gigi's turn. Okay? Okay."

Liza hefted the little girl onto her. Her ankle and leg screamed in protest, but she ignored the pain and retook Gigi's hand. It didn't take them too much longer to reach the grove of thick trees where the oldest girl had said she was going to go.

"Where's Jenni?" one of the girls asked. Liza couldn't make them all out in the dark.

"She's coming. But we need to keep moving. Now—"

"Wait."

The desperate whisper came from behind. Snapping twigs and an approaching form too small to be a Son.

"Jenni!" Bette cried out. Liza immediately clapped her hand over the girl's mouth, but the damage was done. The name echoed out through the trees and if anyone was looking for them, they would have heard that.

"We have to run, girls," Liza ordered, hoping they all understood how important it was to follow directions and ask questions later. "As quietly as possible. You're going to follow me. No sounds. Walk as quietly as possible. We'll walk two by two. Make sure you're holding someone's hand so no one falls back.

Jamison will…" Liza's heart sank when she realized the girl had come alone. "Where's Jamison?" she asked of Jenni, as calmly as possible for the kids' sake.

Jenni let out a ragged sob. "He told me to run. I don't know… I don't know what happened after that."

"That's okay. That's all right," Liza said, though her throat got tight at the thought of him stuck back there in the stables. "You did just what you should have. Now, everyone, find a partner."

They had to get to safety, and to Cody. Because someone had to save Jamison.

She made sure the girls all had a buddy, and settled Jenni at the back with Bette. She began their walk, Gigi's hand in hers, keeping the pace quick and efficient. She tried not to think about Jamison, but it was impossible. With every look back to make sure all the girls were keeping up, she looked beyond, desperate to see Jamison running behind them.

He'd be okay. She assured herself over and over again. Even if he was caught, he was Ace Wyatt's son. No one would hurt him.

At least until Ace got there.

Chapter Sixteen

Jamison hadn't followed into the woods like he'd promised the girl he would. Like he'd promised Liza he would. Still, he'd known Jenni would follow Liza. No matter how unsure she was of him and his promises of safety, she would follow her sister—the little girl Liza had taken away with Gigi.

So, he didn't feel so bad about staying behind. The girls needed more time to escape. This would have all been for nothing if the Sons men discovered they were missing and immediately found them in the woods.

Then there was the fact it would take him time to scale that gate—too much time. He'd only be found.

So, Jamison stayed, and he waited. With luck, there wouldn't be too many coming to bring the girls supper and he could take them out. It would buy everyone time—including himself.

With time he could potentially fashion something out of his backpack to haul himself over the gate or pick the padlock. But only if he had time.

He heard noises. Footsteps, talking. The clank of a chain, the echoing click of a padlock falling open.

He surveyed the room the girls had been in. Somehow he had to take an undetermined amount of men out before they alerted everyone in that house there was a problem.

More chains clinking, then footsteps coming closer.

Jamison positioned himself in a crouch in the corner of darkness the girls had been huddled in. He held his gun in one hand, considering acoustics and wondering if it would send men from the cabin running out here.

It wasn't his best option, but if it was the last resort, so be it.

If there were too many for Jamison to fight, well, he had a plan for that, too.

They hadn't discussed it, but Jamison was counting on Cody still having and monitoring the device connected to the one he'd given Jamison. He was *counting* on Cody understanding that if he hit the button again, it was an okay to blow it all up.

If it blew up with Jamison in the cross fire, so be it. He'd have done what he came to do.

Saving people meant being willing to lay your life down for them if the situation called for it. He'd saved himself a lot of times, and always been willing to pay a bigger price if necessary. This situation couldn't be any different.

Even if a future with Liza was waiting on the other end, it was just as she'd said. How would he live with himself if he didn't give those girls a fighting chance at survival?

He couldn't.

Jamison listened, focusing on the now. Two sets of footsteps. Two voices.

He could definitely take out two men. Maybe even without firing a shot. Still, he held the gun in one hand, a knife in the other, and kept himself ready to attack.

"Learned to be real quiet, haven't they?" a deep voice laughed, coming closer and closer.

"I guess they're smarter than we thought."

That two men could be so callous about keeping little girls locked in a dank, dirty stable had fury spiking through him. Jamison banked the rage and disgust. Had to, in order to focus.

Two big men entered, chuckling to each other as they hung a camping lantern from a hook on the wall. One carried containers of food, and the other held a lamp, with a gun at the ready in his other hand.

"I guess they are smarter than you thought," Jamison said calmly. "Way smarter."

The man with the food immediately dropped it, presumably to reach for a weapon. Jamison lunged—not at either man, but at the light. He smashed the butt of his gun into the plastic and heard a satisfying crunch and shatter before it went out—plunging them into darkness.

They wouldn't shoot blindly into the dark. He had to hope.

Unfortunately, he hoped wrong. The deafening

pop of a gunshot went off, though as far as Jamison could tell, the bullet only hit wood.

"You idiot. You could have killed me," one man said to the other.

"What else am I supposed to do?"

Their arguing gave Jamison time to slip out, his eyes adjusting to the dark as he strode as silently as possible down the stables. He stopped at the stall with the horse. It would make noise, but he could outrun the goons still bickering in the room behind him.

He pulled the horse into the corridor and then gave its rump a hard pat, which had the horse galloping for the front door, where the men had presumably come in.

Jamison didn't give himself time to hope. He just acted, moving through the corridor and then sliding out the door after the horse. He heard the men coming, so he quickly shut the door, pulled the chain through the handles of the door as tightly as possible, then slammed the padlock into place. All by the bright, silver moonlight.

The men no doubt had walkies, and Jamison wished he could have disabled those. But he'd gotten out. Two men were detained, and they wouldn't be able to tell much about which direction he'd gone.

So, Jamison had to move, and quick.

But when Jamison turned away from the door, there was someone standing there. The figure's teeth flashed in the moonlight, and not a second later two men grabbed either arm, liberating both the gun and the knife from his grasp.

Jamison struggled against them, but they had tight grasps, and used their bulk to keep him mostly immobile.

"You honestly think I let idiots like that do anything without listening to their every move?" the voice asked.

A bright light flashed against Jamison's face. Jamison didn't wince at the light, and he forced himself not to tense under the hands of the men who held him down. He had to keep his body loose. It would be his only chance of fighting off the men who gripped him by each arm.

The man in front of him didn't drop the light, so Jamison calmly closed his eyes against it. He didn't have to see to recognize the voice of the man standing before him. "Tony. Good to see you. So to speak, since you're blinding me."

Tony laughed, and Jamison tried not to sneer in response. He'd always hated Liza's father, as much as if not even more than his own. Ace was the leader because he was cold and calculated. He knew how to manipulate, and how to stir up a certain kind of loyalty. He was dangerous because he understood people, and he used that knowledge against them.

Tony Dean was dangerous in the completely opposite way. He didn't care about people. His brain didn't work like other people's—it was incomprehensible as far as Jamison was concerned. Jamison would have called him a sadist, but that would be ascribing his chaos to some kind of order.

No one ever knew quite what Tony was going to

do—which was why he was Ace's right-hand man. The machine and the maniac who'd built quite the kingdom for themselves.

"They won't get far," Tony offered, tilting the flashlight's beam down at the ground so it no longer shone in Jamison's eyes. "But I'm impressed. You certainly got them farther than I expected. Then again, Ace taught you everything you know."

Jamison smiled at Liza's father, though he wanted to retch at the comparison. He wasn't Ace, but Ace *had* taught him something. You couldn't escape the Sons.

And since he wouldn't give in to them, there was only one other choice. Destroying them. Maybe the odds were stacked against him, but he wasn't dead yet.

"Didn't he just?" Jamison returned.

The men held his arms—but with the right shifting on his feet and pressure of his elbow against his pocket, he could put pressure on the button Cody had given him.

He managed to click it once before the men tightened their hold and ordered him to stop moving. He let himself relax, counted to five, then gave a jerk and managed to click the button the second time.

It earned him an elbow to the gut, but if Cody got the message, it was worth the pain and loss of breath.

"Tie him up," Tony said in a heavy sigh. "Don't rough him up too much. We've got Ace Wyatt's precious eldest."

Jamison didn't fight the men at his sides as one

produced a rope from the dark. There was no point in fighting when it would only take Cody a few moments to follow the cue. Jamison hoped.

It took another minute or two. But before Tony's goons had finished tying him up, the first bright light exploded from the cabin, followed by a thunderous, deafening boom and debris flying.

Tony's goons scattered, dropping Jamison's arms and running away from the light.

But Tony didn't. He held the gun on Jamison's half-tied-up form. "I guess you should have set that off a while ago."

"You think so?" Jamison replied cheerfully. "Good to know."

"You think who your father is matters to me? I'm his *partner.* I'm not afraid of Ace. Ace wouldn't mind if I killed you. He'd probably thank me."

"I wouldn't be so sure, Tony." Tony was clearly all talk because he still hadn't pulled the trigger. "I'd think very long and hard before you spoke for my father. You know how he gets."

Another building exploded—this time the shack. Jamison had to believe the stables would be next.

It'd probably kill him. He had to let out a breath and accept that. As long as it took out Tony Dean, too, it would be worth it.

THEY WERE GETTING AWAY. Liza should feel relief. Hope. But her stomach was in knots and she couldn't help but look back every few minutes, hoping to see Jamison catching up with them.

But he didn't.

Most of the girls didn't make a sound as they hiked along in the dark. The farther they got away from the cabin, the more Liza let the pace slow. The girls were tired, likely undernourished no matter how much supper they'd been given, and most of all, terrified.

Liza carried Gigi after a while, Jenni carrying Bette, who appeared to be her little sister. The older girls helped the younger girls. A few times Liza got turned around, but she kept moving forward. She had to believe she'd find the cabin or safety—as long as she was leading them away from the Sons, everything was okay.

Somehow, Jamison would eventually show up. Somehow, she would get the girls to Cody and he would get them all to safety.

Somehow, because her life had always been a series of somehows and she was still here. Still breathing, no matter how much her ankle throbbed or her lungs burned with exertion.

She pushed forward into a clearing, and found her next somehow.

Somehow they'd made it. The cabin sat in the eerie dark of predawn, where it was still dark but the sky seemed to glow.

She'd led the girls to the cabin. She'd saved Gigi. She hugged her sister closer and gathered the girls closer. Relief was a balm, but it was short-lived.

It isn't over yet.

No, no, it wasn't. She couldn't forget that. Even

if she wanted to. Jamison missing left a hard weight of dread in her stomach.

Was he trying to fight them off? Was he lost?

Is he dead?

Even though that question kept swirling around in her head, every time it hit her square, she had a hard time sucking in a breath or letting one out.

Cody stepped out of the cabin as Liza brought the girls into the clearing. He opened his mouth as if to greet them, but as his eyes traveled over the eleven girls, his expression changed.

The girls quickly huddled together, and then behind Liza as much as they could.

"It's all right," she said, looking at Cody. He'd been something like thirteen the last time she'd seen him. Even when he'd spoken to Jamison earlier, she'd only seen a shadow, the hint of a man.

Now she could trace all the similarities to Jamison on his face. His nose wasn't crooked in the same way, and his eyes were lighter—tinged with green. He was more rangy, not quite as broad, but taller.

But, boy, was he a Wyatt. Not only did he have the same appearance as his brothers, it was the expression in them that solidified what she'd begun to accept. She didn't have any doubts about Cody's involvement with the Sons anymore. That look was all cop.

"This is Cody," Liza said. Though she was talking to the girls, she kept her gaze on Cody. Wanted to watch his face and make sure he understood what he was seeing. "He's Jamison's brother. He's going to help us, just like Jamison helped you all out of the stables."

"Let's get you all inside," Cody said. He tried to smile, but he wasn't very good at it. He kept his hands behind his back, though, and stepped clear of the door as if to say to the girls he wasn't a threat. Liza encouraged the girls to go inside, following them like a sheepdog herding its flock.

When she reached the doorway, Cody stopped her. She looked down at his hand on her arm, then gave him a raised-eyebrow look that said "Watch yourself." He might not be with the Sons, but that didn't mean she trusted him.

He didn't budge.

"Sit wherever you like," Cody told the girls as they stood in a group in the middle of the cabin. "You can't do anything wrong in here. You're safe now. Have a seat. Rest." There was a fire in the hearth and a few camping lanterns strewed about. There was also that computer from the bathroom sitting on the counter.

"I'll see what food I can scrounge up in just a moment," Cody continued, his hand on Liza's arm still keeping her from entering.

He nodded at the girls, then closed the door a little bit—leaving it ajar. She didn't want to give him credit, but he seemed to understand the girls wouldn't want to be locked up in another dark place.

"Where's Jamison?" Cody asked quietly, his fingers tightening around her arm.

Liza tried to jerk it away, but he held fast. "Listen—"

"Tell me where he is," Cody seethed.

And because she knew Jamison well enough, she thought she saw something more than anger and a cop on a power trip. Something like fear lurked in Cody's hazel eyes.

"He helped get the girls out, but he…" She swallowed, because she wouldn't believe it meant anything bad. Not yet. "He didn't follow the last one out. He told her he would, but he didn't."

"Liza, are you telling me he isn't… He's not with you? He's back there at the cabin?"

"At the stables. The girls were in the stables. He probably just stayed to make sure we got away. There were men coming and—"

Cody swore and rubbed a hand over his face.

"What? What is it? What's wr—"

Something boomed in the distance, followed by a flash of light.

Everything inside Liza froze as she watched the blaze bloom and grow. "What was that?" she whispered.

"Liza." Cody's voice was careful. Too careful as he slowly released her arm.

"What was that, Cody?" she demanded, giving him a shove. Even though she knew. Even though she knew exactly what it was.

And what it meant.

"He hit the button twice."

"What? What does that mean? What are you talking about?"

Cody heaved out a sigh—irritation, fear, sadness. "I gave him a device. It sends me a message that can't be picked up or intercepted. He hit it once at first, which meant he'd found people in the stables." Cody looked at the door, shaking his head. "Those girls were in there."

"You didn't know."

"I should have," he muttered. "I didn't engage the explosives. I was having a conversation with my superiors about the potential for collateral damage when I got the transmission again—this time twice. That was the signal to engage the explosives."

"For the cabin," Lisa said, more desperate hope than rational thought.

"Liza…"

She didn't wait for him to continue. She turned and started to run back from where she came. Her ankle screamed and she didn't care. Didn't dare worry about her own pain when Jamison was…

"You can't go running into an explosion," Cody called after her. "They'll go off before—" Another boom, more light.

She stopped, looked in horror at what was clearly fire in the dark distance. No. She refused to let this be it. She could get to him. If he'd hit the button, he wasn't stupid enough to be in there getting blown up. No. It wasn't possible.

She didn't get more than a few more strides before Cody grabbed her from behind. She turned and swung a fist at him, but he easily dodged it before grabbing that arm, too, and holding her immobile.

She tried to fight him off, but he held firm.

"You have to stay here with the girls," he said between gritted teeth as she continued to struggle and he maintained his iron hold to keep her in place. "I'll go and—"

"I can't save them, Cody. I've done what I can do. I can't get them to safety from here. You can. You can get men in here or get them out or…something. You have the connections and the computer. You have superiors to communicate with. You have to get them away from here."

"You can't save Jamison if he can't save himself. Liza. He's a trained police officer." There was a pause, and when Cody continued, his voice was flat. "If he didn't survive, there's nothing we can do."

"That's bull." She stilled, then gave up fighting him off, sucked in a ragged breath and let it out. She believed Jamison could survive almost anything, but she also believed she was the same.

She'd needed help sometimes, and Jamison needed help sometimes. He hadn't liberated all his brothers on his own. He'd needed help from his grandmother, from the occasional Sons member who wasn't so keen on hurting kids, sometimes even on strangers.

"Maybe he got out," Cody said, and his tone was almost gentle, perhaps because he had to hope for the same. "Maybe he'll make it here. But you can't go after him. We don't know what's left out there and there's still one more blast to go off."

She didn't want to hear it. Couldn't accept it. "Stop it!" She tried to free her hands so she could reach out and shake him, but he wouldn't release his grip.

"I can't stop it, Liza. If I could, I would have already done it. The explosives are connected. The third one will go off any second. It gave Jamison time—if he ran away after the first blast, he'll have time to get here. You should stay here and wait for him to show up."

"And if he doesn't?"

"That's why you need to let me go. I'll call my guys to come in and get you and the girls out. Then I'll head out and you stay here and safe. Let Wyatts handle Wyatts."

Wyatts handle Wyatts. Jamison was as much hers as anyone's. Beyond that, her father had been the one in the center of this. Not theirs. "But Ace Wyatt wasn't keeping these girls, was he?"

Cody's expression shuttered, going into full cop mode now. She'd hoped he might loosen his grip on her hands, but he held firm.

"Go inside, Liza. I'll handle the rest."

"Be a good little woman and let the big, strong men handle it?" She thought about stomping on his instep, but he shifted, almost as if he could read her thoughts, so that she'd have to do it with her bad ankle.

"Let law enforcement agents handle it."

"Just what *agency* are you with, Cody?"

He shook his head, refusing to answer.

"That's what I thought." Because Cody might have some cop training, but computers and explosives were something else altogether. He might be on the right side, but that didn't mean he was on the right side of the *law*.

When the third explosion went off, she knew she didn't have time to argue. Cody still held her arms. She just needed to escape. She *needed* to do what she could to help Jamison.

She looked up at Cody, letting all the worry and fear show in her eyes. "Sorry about this," she whispered.

"About wh—"

She kneed him in the crotch, using the moment of surprise and pain to wriggle away from his grasp and run like hell.

She reached the edge of the woods before she felt someone grip the back of her coat and yank hard—hard enough she *fell* backward. She glared up at Cody but got right to her feet. He wanted to try to stop her? *Let him.*

She squared, fists clenched and ready to deck him. She'd fight tooth and nail to have a chance to save Jamison.

He rolled his eyes. Insultingly. "You're out of your mind."

"What does that make him?" Liza gritted out, keeping her fists up and ready. Cody had already let his guard down once. He'd do it again and she'd land a decent enough punch. Again and again, until she got to Jamison.

But in two seconds flat he moved, like a ghost or a ninja, and had both her hands behind her back with one hand and snaked his other arm around her throat.

"It makes him completely insane," Cody said with disgust. "Now, get ahold of yourself and I'll let you go."

"You'll *what*?"

"I'll let you go. I just need you to let me do something first."

"I'm not going to fall for any tri—"

"You've got to stop," Cody muttered. He started grumbling about people who wouldn't follow orders and how this was life-and-death, on and on. But she'd stilled, and as he grumbled, he shoved something up her sleeve.

"There. Now, go ahead on your fool's errand. But when you end up dead, don't come haunting me. I warned you."

She stared at her sleeve. "What did you do?"

"Don't worry about it. Trust me."

"Why should I trust you?"

"I'm assuming because we both love Jamison and don't want him to be dead."

Liza blinked at that, then scowled when Cody made a shooing motion. "Go on, now. I've got to deal with the girls you saved. Just trust that if you find Jamison, I'll be able to send someone to find you both. All you have to do is stay alive."

The girls you saved. Because she'd gotten Gigi out, gotten her safe. Cody had explosives and contacts and would be able to get law enforcement in here to get those girls somewhere safe—so she'd done her duty to her sister.

Now she had to do her duty to the man she'd always loved, who'd saved her once upon a time. Because she'd saved those girls, and she was going to save him, too.

Chapter Seventeen

There was pain. Everywhere. Pulsing, searing, burning. He wanted to float away from it all, but there
was something he needed to do. Somewhere he
needed to be.

Jamison managed to blink his eyes open, only to
find flame. Everywhere.

It was the fire—that clear reminder of what had
happened—that had him leaping to his feet no matter how his body and balance protested. He stumbled
a little to the left, trying to right himself before he
fell over and only just barely succeeding.

He searched the world around him. Everything
was on fire—or at least so it seemed. He ordered
himself to calm, to catalog. The blast had thrown
him some and he wasn't as close to the stables as
he'd been. Now that he was on his feet, he could see
that the spots of fire were where debris had landed
and smoldered.

In one of those spots of fire lay a body. Not too
far off from Jamison himself. Jamison took a few
stilted steps toward it.

Tony Dean lay completely still, eyes open and unseeing, a gruesome piece of debris sticking out of his gut.

Jamison stared at the body for more time than he had, trying to reconcile…any of what had happened. Tony Dean was dead, and somehow Jamison was alive.

There was no time for contemplating that, though. He had to find…safety. Water. Fresh air. He had to get away from this place because he could hear shouts, see shadows of men trying to put out the blaze.

It hadn't taken down everyone.

Liza's father and surely the men Jamison had left in the stables were dead. Maybe the men who'd tried to tie him up, but maybe not—they'd started running after the first blast. Which would have definitely killed the men who'd been inside the cabin at the time, but Jamison could see at least eight men running around house and shack. Their focus was on putting out the fire, as far as Jamison could tell.

He began to walk, though every part of his body throbbed in painful protest. He moved for the woods. He wanted to believe that everyone would be too busy with the flames to look for him, but he knew the Sons.

He knew what kind of orders Tony would have given his men before he'd gone out to meet Jamison at the stables. Tony had known it was him. It would have been imperative for Tony to spread the message that the person who'd liberated those girls was none other than Ace Wyatt's son.

Someone would be looking for him once the confusion died down.

Jamison had to be gone by that time, and not toward the cabin where Liza had been headed. That could lead the wrong people toward Liza and those poor girls. He wasn't sure how much time he'd been unconscious for, but it couldn't have been that long if the flames and shouts were anything to go by.

Not enough time for Cody to have helped Liza and those girls to safety.

Jamison swore under his breath and had to hope against hope that his brother would prioritize the girls and not come running after him once he realized Jamison had sent the signal while still on the premises.

Jamison found the woods behind the wreckage of the stables. Some of the trees were on fire. He skirted the line of trees and the fire and moved toward the front of the cabin. He'd go that way—the complete opposite of the direction he'd come.

He tried to bring the map to his mind, picturing where he'd be going if he headed out that way. How he could get to safety and help in that direction. Everything was a little fuzzy—clearly he was more rattled from the explosion and his loss of consciousness than he wanted to admit.

Rattled or not, he had to keep moving. There was no time for stopping to clear his head and *think*. He couldn't afford to be seen or caught. Not in such bad shape. He wouldn't stand a chance in a fight right now.

He made it toward the front of the burning cabin. The explosion had impacted the back side of the house the most, so anyone trying to stop the fire was back there. The front seemed empty.

But there was a road here. A road Jamison didn't remember being on his map—though it was dirt, so maybe that was why. If he was going to go in the opposite direction of where Liza had taken the girls, he had to cross this road with no cover.

Something in his body recoiled from the idea. He pushed it away, chalking it up to explosions and head fuzziness and the odd shakes now racking his body. Just shock or adrenaline or something. He moved forward, feeling as though he was pushing through molasses.

Something wasn't right, but he didn't have *time*. On the next step, his leg gave out and he fell to his knee. He looked down in surprise at the offending limb. It was only then he realized he had his own dagger of debris stuck in his calf and he was just now noticing the pain, the blood dripping down into his boot.

That couldn't be good. Worse when all he could seem to do was stare at the piece of wood, not sure what to do about it.

The sound of an engine brought him out of his reverie. He spotted a Jeep cresting the hill. Also not good.

Jamison tried to jump out of the way as the headlights got closer, but his body wasn't moving at full capacity. The light caught him. Jamison moved to run, but another car came—and men materialized from the woods until he was surrounded.

He stood, breathing heavily, unable to think of one smart action to take.

The door of the first Jeep opened and out stepped his father, the flames dancing across his smiling face. A face all too similar to the one Jamison saw in the mirror.

Jamison actually laughed. It was so ridiculous. So impossible. All the things he could survive and in the end it would still come back to this moment right here.

Maybe it was fitting.

"You're not looking too good, son," Ace said with a smirk.

"And, per usual, Ace Wyatt is unharmed and unscathed. Go figure." There were six men creating a perimeter around Jamison, all with semiautomatic guns pointed at his chest. They wouldn't shoot—unless given the okay from Ace, or maybe if Jamison went after Ace. Then all bets would be off.

No, they wouldn't kill him, but they wouldn't be afraid to hurt him if he ran, either.

Jamison thought running and risking getting hurt might be worth the chance of escape. But if Tony was dead and Ace was here, staying put and keeping Ace busy meant a better chance for Liza and the girls to get away. The longer he could keep his father's attention on *him*, the better for *them*.

"So. Is this how it ends, Dad? Or do we get to have a heart-to-heart first?" Jamison had to work to keep his teeth from chattering.

"Jamison, you underestimate me. It's never the end until someone's on their knees, begging."

"I've never underestimated you. I have had a few fantasies about you on your knees, begging."

Ace laughed. "The sad thing is, even if you could make that happen, you'd never have the balls to pull the trigger. Too much of your mother in you. She had her chances to end me, and she never could."

Jamison didn't explode like he might have years ago. One thing he'd learned about his father was that he only ever brought up Mom when Jamison was actually getting to him.

So, Jamison pushed the old hurt away, let the cold shock of *all* of this make his words lifeless and bored. "You still sticking by that drug overdose story? Or did you want to confess?"

"The thing about you, Jamison, and why you've never been any threat to me, is you're too *good* to understand how the world works. I know you weren't behind this." He waved a hand to encompass the flames. "You don't have it in you. All this collateral damage, death. It'd eat you alive."

Jamison considered all the people who'd been inside the burning cabin, involved or complicit in eleven little girls—*girls*—being held captive in the stables. He had no doubt the whispers Liza had heard were correct. The girls were here to be trafficked—and likely weren't the first group of girls.

"That might have been true once," Jamison replied. "It isn't true any longer."

"Tell me, Jamison, why is it a child's life is so much more precious to you than anyone else's? Don't we all have souls? Don't we all have the capacity to change?"

"You have a choice in everything you do. Children don't." It came out edgier than he wanted it to. His body was shaking against his will and he was beginning to fully understand he couldn't make it out of this situation alive.

That had been fine enough when he'd been sacrificing himself to end something. It wasn't so fine if his father got to do it the way he'd always wanted to.

"Everyone who can walk and talk has a choice, Jamison. I was seven years old when I was left on my own to die, but I chose to live. To lead. Just like you chose the coward's escape, and a sad little life trying to feel important because of a badge."

It might have pricked at his pride some, but not enough to bite. His escape hadn't been cowardly, and it wasn't his badge that made him feel important. It was the fact that some days, he did get to help people. Some days, he was all that stood between a person and harm. Maybe not as many days as he'd anticipated when he'd been going through the academy.

But enough. Helping was always enough.

If things ended here, at his father's hands, he'd saved eleven little girls' lives, and that was a price he was willing to pay. Always.

THE CLOSER LIZA GOT, the larger the flames seemed. Still, she didn't let that slow her steps. Until she saw a body lying still as death. She exhaled shakily, then forced herself to inhale. To calm. She stepped forward, determined to keep it together.

She held her composure and checked to make sure it wasn't Jamison.

It wasn't.

The wave of relief almost took her to her knees, but it was hardly over yet. There was more walking to do. And more bodies on the ground.

The next body she checked wasn't Jamison, either, but still her heart lurched.

It was her father. There were pieces of debris sticking out of him, and part of his body was burned. His eyes were open and unseeing. He was very clearly dead.

She didn't feel sad so much as horrified. Growing up in the Sons meant she'd seen a dead body before. She'd watched men shoot each other. She understood death a little too intimately, and to an extent she'd learned to detach herself from it. Had to in order to survive.

But this was her father.

She'd hated him for as long as she could remember, but it was her own eyes that stared back at her. She could hate him, and what he did, but it didn't make the feelings inside her uncomplicated.

She leaned down and closed his eyes and let out a breath to steady herself. It was good. He couldn't hurt anyone anymore. Not her. Not Gigi. No more Carlees—at least not by his hand. Good riddance.

As she moved to stand back up, she noticed a few things on the ground. Jamison's backpack, for one. It wasn't guaranteed that meant Jamison had been out here. Dad could have taken it off Jamison inside the stables, left Jamison there to die and brought the pack outside.

But Jamison's headlamp was also on the ground a few feet away, as if it had been knocked off him. Which meant Jamison hadn't been in the stables when the explosion had gone off. They might have taken his backpack from him, but they would have destroyed the headlamp, not moved it out here.

She stood, believing these signs meant Jamison was alive. Desperately needing to believe it. She walked on, checking every body she found, avoiding the cluster of men standing next to the flames of the cabin.

They seemed to be conferring, and if they were worried about strangers infiltrating their grounds, they certainly didn't act it.

Jamison wasn't dead. He couldn't be dead. She would have seen him in the wreckage. She would *feel* it. So, she had to keep looking, keep trying to find him wherever he'd gone.

She crept forward. If Jamison had escaped all these men, he would have gone in the opposite direction of where she'd taken the girls. Too much potential to be followed if he came back to Cody's cabin.

He would have gone this way, hoping if he was

caught or followed, they'd have no idea the girls had gone the opposite direction. He would do everything to keep the Sons off her tail.

Maybe she should backtrack. He wasn't dead as far as she could tell, and he wasn't hurt if he was on the move. She should go back to Cody's cabin and let him find her.

No matter how many times her brain urged her to do that, her body could only seem to move forward listening to the crackle of the fire, the conversations of small groups of men. Looking out for bodies, and always seeing Jamison's face a second before she realized—no, that was not him.

She paused as she reached the front area of the cabin. There were a few vehicles circled in the front drive, all with their headlights pointing to the same spot.

Everything inside her stilled as she focused on the spot where all the light was directed.

In the center of it all was Jamison.

And Ace.

Jamison looked awful. Bloody and singed, a gruesome piece of wood sticking out of his leg. Six men stood around them with very large-looking weapons. All pointed at Jamison.

Liza swallowed and looked down at her sleeve. Whatever Cody had put there or done, she had no idea. But he said he'd be able to find them.

They had to be alive for it to matter. Liza crept closer. There was no way she could take all six men. She wouldn't even be able to create a diversion.

They'd just kill her. If she was lucky they'd *just* kill her.

"Let's not do this here," she heard Ace say. He sounded amiable, almost like he was having a pleasant business discussion.

Cold dread formed at the base of her spine, making it hard to move or think. She knew that tone of voice. And she knew the kind of orders that came after it.

Kill him.

But she knew, she *knew*, Ace wouldn't kill Jamison—right away. He'd torture him first, get his poetic revenge. Liza stood to her full height, even as her body shook. If she were there, they'd torture her first. He'd want to make Jamison watch.

As much as she didn't want to put him through that, it would keep him alive. She needed time. Time for Cody to track them however he thought he could track them. So, she couldn't let Jamison go it alone.

She cleared her throat and slowly stepped toward the beams of light. "Having some kind of party, Ace? And you didn't invite me?" Her voice was light, even if her hands shook.

Jamison swore viciously. She smiled at him. He didn't smile back, but at least he was smart enough—or maybe just hurt enough—not to go on.

"Ah, the Juliet to my son's Romeo. Touching that you'd want to die with him, Liza. Really."

One of the armed men nudged her into the circle of light. She looked at Ace with a sharp smile. "I take it you've never actually *read* Shakespeare."

Ace inclined his head and one of his men stepped forward and plowed his fist into her jaw. She saw stars, but she kept her balance. She'd been taking blows since she'd been a kid.

Of course, Jamison lunged at the man, idiot that he was, and got knocked to the ground by the butt of a gun.

Liza crouched next to him. "Don't. I can take it," she whispered, letting her fingers drift gently over his temple. He was dirty and bloody, and she wanted so badly to hold on to him. She looked at Ace. She had to keep the attention off Jamison. The more Ace decided to torture her, the better chance they had.

Jamison couldn't take much more beating from the look of it—he was clearly in shock. So, Liza stood, helping Jamison to his feet.

"What are you doing?" he choked out.

She only shook her head at him. "Ace likes watching *other* men beat up women and little girls because deep, deep down he's a coward." She shot Ace another screw-you smile.

"A coward." Ace laughed, but there was a sneer to it. Not so easy to dismiss her when she was poking at his pride. "I see your father didn't knock near enough sense into you."

"My father's dead." She matched his sharp smile with one of her own. "Saw him myself. What are you going to do without Tony to carry out your sadistic punishments you can't stomach yourself?"

He withered, and Liza felt a certain kind of triumph

light her up from the inside. She was getting to him—which was quite a feat.

She'd probably end up dead because of it, but it was satisfying one way or another.

"You think he's the only sick bastard ready to jump to do my bidding, Liza." Ace sighed as if she was a particularly dim-witted child. "Surely you didn't think your father was special. I'll replace him once I've killed both of you." He snapped his fingers. "Like that."

"You've had so much time to kill us, Ace. Yet here we still are. Chatting."

"Tie her up. And gag her, for the love of God."

Two of the men grabbed her. She decided to fight them, because it would take more time. When one hit his gun against the back of her head, she didn't just see stars, the world went black for a second. She clung to consciousness, but she stopped fighting.

They tied her up roughly, shoved a gag in her mouth with even more force. Her vision had doubled, but slowly came back to clarity.

Jamison was watching her, murder in his eyes. She realized she'd miscalculated more than she cared to admit, because with that look on his face he was going to get himself killed long before help came.

"You do pose a very interesting question, though, Liza. One, I assume, has kept you both up at night." Ace smiled again. "Many nights. For many years. Is that shadow going to materialize into everything I ran away from?"

Ace moved toward Liza. She refused to let fear

grip her because it would show up on her face. When Ace took her chin in his hand, though, she couldn't help but recoil.

He watched her with a glint she knew too well. She'd seen that look so many times over the years on her father's face. A man who enjoyed inflicting pain on people.

She'd never seen Ace actually hurt anyone. Order someone else to kill or torture, yes, but she'd never seen him do the dirty work. She wasn't so sure she'd be able to say the same after tonight—if she'd ever be able to say anything at all.

"You want to know why you both survived as long as you did? Because, Liza, you're less than nothing. No one cares about you, so hurting you doesn't help me any. Or didn't."

He turned his gaze to Jamison, though he kept his hand on her face. "I was waiting for you to have a son, Jamison. So, I could take him away from you like you took mine away from me. I know you don't value your own life, but you would have valued a child's." His gaze returned to Liza. "And it appears you value hers now. That's good to know."

He released Liza's chin and walked toward one of the cars. "Take that stick out of my son's leg, then put them both in my Jeep," he ordered one of his men. "Don't communicate anything over the walkie. Follow my driver."

All Liza could think was, *Please, Cody, hurry.*

Chapter Eighteen

They were both going to die.

Jamison could come up with no other possible outcome of being shoved into his father's vehicle. Hurt, probably as injured as he'd ever been. His father was going to win.

Scratch that. There had to be a way he could save Liza. Had to be. He couldn't give up on her. He'd saved too many people under next-to-impossible circumstances because he'd believed he could. This wouldn't be any different.

One of his father's other goons pushed Liza in on the opposite side. Dad and his driver sat up front and conferred about something, but Jamison couldn't hear.

Maybe once the Jeep got going, one of them could open the door and jump out. They'd maybe die, or be hurt enough to eventually die, but it would be better than whatever Ace was cooking up.

Jamison wasn't tied up like Liza. He'd love to believe it was out of stupidity, but no doubt Ace had some sick reason for the lack of restraint. Maybe to give them hope. Maybe he wanted them to try to escape so he could make the game last. Maybe he knew Jamison just didn't have it in him to fight.

But he'd find a way. Someway.

If there was anything Jamison understood about his father, it was that he liked the long game. Some people grew up suffering, and when they pulled themselves out of it they wanted to help end others' suffering. So, no one had to go through what they had. Jamison understood that one.

Others, like Ace, grew up and out of their desperate circumstances wanting to inflict that pain on someone else—and those people almost always escalated—inflicting more and more of that pain. And then even more.

Still, Jamison calculated the odds. He could disable his father's driver with one well-timed blow, which could cause an accident. Of course, Ace and his driver were buckled—Jamison and Liza were not. Survival wasn't in their favor.

As he went through several other scenarios, Liza inched her way over on the back seat. Despite her hands being tied around her back, she maneuvered herself until she could reach her fingers out to brush against his hand.

He took her hand in his, then tested the bonds. He could untie them. It would give them more of a chance.

Her fingers curled around his and squeezed, and she shook her head.

Jamison knew he couldn't talk, couldn't risk his

father overhearing anything, but it just about killed him to keep his mouth shut.

Then she started to…tap his palm. At first he thought she was trying to get his attention, but she already had it. There were pauses between the taps. Hard taps and light taps. Not Morse code…or any code he knew.

But Cody had done that. Cody, who had access to things. Was she trying to tell him that Cody was going to help them?

Liza was here without the girls, which meant she'd gotten them somewhere safe—Cody. Cody had the girls, and Cody potentially had the means to save them. Potentially.

He supposed he had to stay alive to find out. Which meant outwitting his father. He'd be stupid to think it would be easy.

But maybe *with* Liza, it could be possible.

"It's real sweet you two found your way back to each other. Real sweet," Ace said, curling his arm behind the driver's seat and turning his body so he could face them. He smiled genially, like a real father might look at his son and his son's girlfriend.

But he was not a real father, no matter how well he could put on the mask of one.

Liza made a noise, but it was muffled by the gag in her mouth. Probably for the best, because she couldn't articulate something snarky to Ace.

"It's a shame about your sister," Ace said, still smiling pleasantly at Liza.

Liza's eyebrows drew together, but since she

couldn't talk, Jamison had to ask the questions. Which was always a minefield when it came to Ace. Still, he couldn't let the information sit there if only because Liza would want answers—and would get them one way or another.

"What do you mean?" Jamison asked, not having to feign confusion.

"I figured you two being here meant you'd figured out she was here." Ace scratched his cheek, seeming to mull that over. Then he shrugged. "She was in the stables. Which means the explosion—which I assume you had something to do with—would have killed her. A real shame you're responsible for the death of your beloved sister, and ten of her closest friends."

Jamison could only stare at his father. He counted his heartbeats to keep from laughing or smiling or anything that might give away the truth.

Ace thought the girls had still been in the stables. Somewhere communication had broken down and he didn't know.

He didn't know.

Jamison wanted to laugh. He wanted to laugh and laugh and laugh.

Even if they didn't escape, as long as Cody found Jamison and Liza, he'd be able to arrest Ace Wyatt for connections to a human trafficking ring.

Liza turned her head into Jamison's shoulder. She didn't make a noise, but she made some effort to move her shoulders as if trying to convince Ace she was crying. Jamison had a feeling she was laughing like he wanted to.

Jamison ducked his own head, pressing his face into her hair. The absolute worst thing they could do was tip Ace off that they'd gotten the girls out, but it gave Jamison such hope it was a hard thing to fight.

Instead he and Liza kept their heads bent together as the Jeep traveled over bumpy roads—if they were even roads they were traveling over. Jamison couldn't see out of the tinted windows, so he didn't bother trying.

When the vehicle stopped, Jamison didn't have to work to hide his smile any longer. Dread crept over all that hope. Whatever happened before hope won, he was going to endure a heck of a lot of hurt before they succeeded.

Dad and his driver got out, then both sides of the back doors opened and two of Dad's men grabbed each of them, jerking them out of the Jeep on opposite sides.

Jamison bit his tongue to keep from crying out as each tug of his limbs felt like fire, but he would do everything not to give them the satisfaction of hurting him.

Liza was still bound and gagged, but since he was pushed up a cement walkway first, Jamison couldn't see if she was fighting the men who were bringing her forward. He had to concentrate on fighting the pain and dizziness so he could stay on his own two feet. His leg had gone numb, which was something of a relief. He limped through the numbness and squinted his eyes through the dizzying swirl of the world around him.

Jamison recognized where they were, sort of. It was Flynn, and a building he'd been in a hundred times as a child. But it wasn't the rotting structure of an old church any longer. It had been fixed up, remodeled or restored. The outside looked like a modest church that was well tended. A pure white against a grove of old trees. It was like stepping into a picture, especially as the sun was rising in the east, pouring gold over the world around them. Like a promise.

There was no peace to be found here, but he wanted to believe that sunrise was the promise of peace he'd find if he held on.

The man holding him shoved him inside the quaint building, and again it was nothing like it had been when Jamison was with the Sons.

The interior was finished and looked like some kind of shrine. Instead of the ruins of an old church Jamison remembered, the pews nearly gleamed like the wood floor. The altar was sweeping and held a big chair in the middle of it, where a pulpit would normally be.

Ace took a seat on the chair.

There weren't any Christian symbols anywhere, but signs of the Sons. Their patch—a skull amid the Badlands—on a flag hanging from one wall, their motto burned into the wood of the wall behind Ace.

The Srong Save Themselves.

Ace sat underneath it, giving the appearance of

royalty, or maybe something larger than royalty. He fancied himself a god, and this would be his church. The Sons were his loyal worshippers.

And the disloyal were punished.

This was something fancier than Jamison had ever seen the Sons put together. It was like Tony's cabin setup—incongruous to the transient, ready-to-move Sons Jamison had grown up a part of.

Had they gotten so bold, so sure they'd never be caught that they'd actually planted roots?

Jamison didn't know whether to be cheered by that, by all it meant for their potential to be caught and brought to justice, or to be scared down to his bones that they were really unstoppable.

No, he'd never believe they were unstoppable. Maybe evil triumphed over good more than it should—but that didn't mean it survived in the same form forever.

There were other sayings burned into the walls. "The strong wear a patch. The weak wear a badge."

Underneath that one were pictures of badges, with specific officers' DSNs either etched into the badge or written underneath. There were red Xs over some.

The police officers they'd killed.

Jamison ignored the white-hot surge of anger and focused on the fact it was evidence to bring them down. He'd seen it now, and if he lived, it could be evidence used to put Ace in jail.

Truly behind bars for the first time ever.

"This is a bit ridiculous, even for you," Jamison

said, earning him a jab from the gun the man behind him held.

"This?" Ace asked, gesturing around the church. "This is your chance to beg my forgiveness, son. Your chance to beg. I'd suggest getting on your knees."

Jamison laughed, then spit at his father. He knew the blow would come, so he dodged it and turned to face the two men with guns behind him. They held the guns trained on him, but they couldn't use them. Not without the nod from Ace.

There were *some* perks to being a madman's son.

"You, get him on his knees," Ace said tightly. "You, bring her here."

The first goon came at Jamison, who elbowed him in the nose, sending a splatter of blood across the gleaming wood floor. It felt a little *too* good—the kind of good that reminded Jamison he was indeed the son of a madman.

He didn't like that feeling, didn't want violence to sing through him, potent and deadly, so nothing else mattered.

Because Liza mattered, and she was being led up to his father. The two men moving her forward didn't force her to kneel—they positioned her on his father's lap, like she was a small child.

Or worse.

Ace smiled at Jamison.

Jamison swallowed down the rage and the bile and lowered himself onto his knees. He would kneel.

He'd even beg. But he wouldn't give up. Not on saving Liza.

"Good boy," Ace said. He curled an arm around Liza's waist. She raised her chin and fixed her gaze forward but didn't react in any other way.

"I was left to die by my own parents, but I didn't die. I survived, and what I built—"

"In my survival is a loyal community ready to do my bidding. Because I was strong. Stronger than anyone," Jamison intoned. He had knelt, but he refused to look at the floor in supplication. He held his father's steely gaze. "Your speeches are still boring and predictable."

"Every true leader must go through betrayals, Jamison. I have been through yours. I've waited for retribution, because a good leader bides his time. A good leader, a true leader waits until the time is right, no matter how long."

"Well, since I don't have any sons for you to steal, I guess you'll have to wait a little longer."

"Transgressions must be paid for, Jamison." His grip on Liza tightened and it took every ounce of control Jamison had honed in thirty-seven years to stay where he was and not lunge at Ace. "One of you will pay with blood. The other will pay with failure."

"You're starting to sound more like a cult than a gang," Jamison gritted out.

"Don't worry," Ace said easily. "We can be both. What happens when a strong leader falls, Jamison? Chaos. What happens if you don't return to your brothers? Would they fall apart, too? No. I don't think so. You'd be their thing to avenge. Vengeance for a particular person can't be your motivation. If I only wanted vengeance on my parents, what would I have built? Nothing. I wanted vengeance on the world and I built one of my own."

"It's a big world out there, outside the Sons. All you've built is a…village, maybe," Jamison returned, because if he kept Ace talking, he bought them all time. Jamison had to believe time mattered.

"I don't need the world, Jamison. I only need the loyal. It's a shame that's neither of you." Dad produced a knife and held it far too close to Liza's cheek. "I taught you that the only truth is power. Everything else is a weakness. You didn't believe me. Now I have your weakness right here. What do you think I should do with it?"

LIZA DID EVERYTHING she could to hide her revulsion. Ace's arm was wrapped around her waist like a python. The contact made her stomach roil in disgust.

She could see the barely leashed fury in Jamison's eyes, and she knew it wouldn't last forever. He'd snap if something didn't change. And soon.

Ace had one thing right, she *was* Jamison's weakness, because he'd likely do something stupid before he let Ace hurt her.

Ace pressed the knife to her cheek, and she moved her gaze to Jamison. She knew he wouldn't see it if he didn't *want* to see it, but she did everything she could with her eyes to beg him to stay put.

"You surprise me," Ace said as the knife pricked

the skin of her cheek. "Either you've learned some restraint or she doesn't mean much to you at all. Both would make me proud."

"That's what I've always lived for," Jamison returned caustically. "To make you proud."

"I know you fancy yourself above my influence, but don't think there isn't something to you becoming a cop. You and all your brothers. As if that badge will save you from what you really are."

The knife dug harder against her cheek, and Liza did everything she could not to react outwardly to the searing pain.

Then, out of nowhere, both the knife and gag dropped from her face.

"I wouldn't want to muffle your screams of pain," Ace said. This time when he pressed the knife to her skin, it was against her throat.

Fear was ice in her veins, but she focused on Jamison. She focused on the battle light in his eyes, in all the ways he'd tried to save her.

But she'd needed to do her own saving. She'd saved Gigi. She could save Jamison.

She wouldn't shake. She wouldn't beg. She would be strong, the way he'd always taught her to be.

"Don't you want to order one of your morons to do the dirty work for you?" she asked, her voice steady, disdainful.

"Normally I would, since you're less than nothing, but I want Jamison to have the vision of me slitting your throat in his head till the day he dies."

Liza knew she couldn't stop herself from being

killed. She was in too deep and death seemed inevitable. But she wouldn't give Ace the satisfaction of having it his way.

He had a knife to her throat and her hands were tied behind her back. Jamison was eyeing the men with guns on him, clearly calculating his own attempt to save her.

If they could act together, it would be more of a fight than a slaughter—but how?

She didn't have time to think up an answer because something exploded behind her, sending her sprawling off Ace's lap and onto the floor—face-first.

She was so dazed it took her a few seconds to realize she was on the floor, people were shouting, guns were going off. She was bleeding—from the cut Ace's knife had made in her cheek, possibly her throat. She wasn't sure. Everything was a blur.

Until someone grabbed her.

Ace flipped her onto her back and she immediately fought back. She didn't have any strategy, just to kick as hard as she could—but she didn't have her hands. She didn't have anything.

He used his body to bracket her legs together. She twisted and fought to sit up, but he held her shoulders down. On the bright side, he couldn't exactly stab her as long as he was holding her down.

"You think you've won," Ace said, moving one hand from her shoulder to the center of her chest. He held her down with that one hand then, brandishing that awful knife. "But you'll never win."

"That's the difference between you and me, Ace. I don't need to win. Surviving this nightmare is enough for me. I don't need more than that."

"You think you're going to survive?" He laughed. "I'm the survivor."

"Not this time," a man's voice said from behind Ace.

Ace stilled and Liza looked up at the figure. Cody held a gun to Ace's head.

Cody was here. But... "The girls..." Liza whispered.

"Are fine and safe," Cody assured her.

Ace's eyebrows drew together for a moment as he looked at the knife in his hand. As he seemed to put together what that could mean.

"Yeah, we saved them," Liza had the pleasure of telling Ace. "Right under your nose. Want to lecture me some more about strong leaders? We've all been stronger than you, Ace. Now you're going to find out how much."

"Drop the knife," Cody ordered.

"I could slit her throat before you put a bullet in my brain, son. I'd watch the tone you take with me."

"Do it, then."

Liza couldn't hide the surprise or horror that stole over her face, especially as Ace looked like he was just about to do that.

But a gunshot went off, and somehow the knife flew out of Ace's hand, clattering to the ground as the bullet crashed into the opposite wall. Someone had *shot* the knife out of Ace's hand.

When Liza stared up at Cody, he shrugged. "Snipers come in handy now and again. As do explosive experts," he said, giving a vague nod toward the blown-in back of the building. He then inclined his head toward someone. Liza felt herself be pulled out from under Ace, the binding on her wrists being cut as she was set on her feet.

She surveyed the very strange sight. Almost the entire back wall of the church, so to speak, was gone, but there wasn't fire left like at the cabin and stables. Explosives expert, indeed.

She glanced at the interior. Two of Ace's men were tied to each other, lying in a heap. Two others were clearly dead. And Jamison... Jamison was lying on the floor—one of Cody's men patching him up.

Liza practically tripped over herself to run to his side.

"I'm all right," he muttered as she reached out to touch his cheek.

"He's got a head wound that needs stitches, at the very least," the person working on him corrected. Liza was surprised the voice belonged to a woman. All of the people Cody had brought in were dressed in head-to-toe black, armed to the teeth and wore a variety of hats, helmets and scarves that obscured their identities down to gender.

She looked back at Cody, wondering what on earth he was involved in. Then back at Jamison.

"Is Ace still alive?" Jamison asked, his voice a raw scrape that had her wincing at the pain it must have caused him.

"I think so."

"Help me up, then," he said, struggling to push himself up as both Liza and the other woman kept him pressed to the floor.

"Jamison."

"You shouldn't get up," the woman said, though she had wrapped a bandage around his head.

"Have to," Jamison said to the woman.

Knowing he wouldn't give up, Liza gave a nod to the woman and helped Jamison to his feet. He swayed as he stood, and Liza helped steady him, then led him over to Cody.

Cody, who still held a gun to Ace's head, had a look on his face that had Liza grabbing onto Jamison's arm—trying to keep him away from this scene. Ace was lying on his back, smiling up at Cody, and nothing—*nothing*—good could come from this moment.

But Jamison calmly put his hand on Cody's shoulder. "Don't kill him."

Chapter Nineteen

Cody didn't look away from Ace's grinning face, but Jamison knew Cody had heard him. His grip on the gun had changed, and there was a sense of hesitation to him now.

Jamison knew he had to press on that while he could. "I want him to rot in a cell," Jamison continued calmly. His head ached, and his vision was gray and doubled, but he was alive. He'd survive.

Now he had to make sure his baby brother did, too. Really *survive*, not just walk out of this alive.

"If he's dead, it's over," Cody said, his finger curled around the trigger. But Ace would already be dead if Cody didn't have a certain level of uncertainty about killing their father.

Over. It was tempting. To know Ace wouldn't be able to pop up in their lives in the future and wreak havoc. Wasn't that what had held him back from really *having* a life all these years?

But Cody would have to live with it, and Jamison didn't think it was worth it. That weight. Forever.

"Do you want to be like him?" Jamison asked quietly.

Cody didn't answer that, so Jamison continued.

"His second-in-command is dead. He'll be going to jail for a very long time." Jamison turned to face his father. If Ace felt defeated, he didn't look it. Jamison wanted him to *look* defeated. To feel it. To embody it. And a jail cell? Jamison was certain the lack of freedom would do just that. Far more than death ever could. "What did you say happens in the absence of a powerful leader, Dad?"

Ace smiled. "Chaos, son."

Jamison nodded and turned back to Cody. "We got what we wanted. This is over. The Sons will be chaos. He'll rot in jail, and you know it. It's over. Don't make it live on for yourself forever."

"It'll never be over, Jamison," Ace said, all but laughing as he spoke. "Not ever. Not until one of you has the guts to take me out. But you won't. None of you have the courage. None of you have the survival instinct."

Jamison watched Cody's jaw work, but he didn't have to say anything. Cody lowered the gun. "You sound like a man who wants to die, Ace. I don't plan to be the one to give you what you want."

Cody made a signal, and two of the men who'd swept in after the explosion pulled Ace to his feet and handcuffed him.

"Not a complaint," Jamison said, watching his father being led away. "But since you all clearly aren't licensed law enforcement, should you be handcuffing him?"

"We'll take care of it," Cody replied. He still held the gun with too tight a grip, and his gaze hadn't left their father. "It'll be legal by the time we're done."

Jamison didn't know how to feel about that.

"The girls?" Liza asked.

Cody finally turned away from Ace and motioned Liza and Jamison to follow him out through the exploded back wall. There were a line of black cars waiting.

"They've been taken to a medical center. I didn't want to get Social Services involved until you were both there. Some of the girls could tell us who their parents were and if they were involved in the Sons, but some are just too young. It's going to take some doing, but we want to make sure we don't return any of these girls to parents who might have sold them."

"Sold them?" Liza said on a gasp.

"Unfortunately, it happens. And in the Sons? Anything is possible. But no matter who's in charge now, we took down almost the entire trafficking ring. Tony is dead. Ace will be incarcerated. It's not likely to happen again. Not here anyway."

"You didn't know the girls were there, though," Jamison said as he followed Cody to the cars. "How did…"

"We were investigating the death of Carlee Bright. She has a connection to someone in our group. We hadn't found any evidence of the trafficking. Which leads me to believe this may have been their first attempt. That you two stopped it before it got off the ground."

"We didn't stop anything," Jamison said. The girls had already been captured. He had no idea how they'd been treated in those stables, or for how long. At best he'd kept them from a worse fate, but he certainly hadn't kept them from fear or cruelty.

"Those girls would be dead if not for you two. We would have blown them up." Cody said that flatly, but Jamison knew that kind of misplaced guilt well enough to recognize it.

He squeezed his brother's shoulder. "But you didn't."

Cody nodded. "My men will take you to the girls. Where you can also be checked out. J, you can get those stitches. Liza can get her ankle looked at. The rest of us have a lot of work to do here and at the other explosion site."

It was a strange thing to be told what to do by his baby brother. At Valiant County, Jamison was the ranking officer. To sit back and let Cody and "his men" take care of it was the antithesis to everything Jamison wanted to do.

But Cody had saved him. Not that he couldn't offer his two cents. "There were badges. Pictures of badges—DSNs x-ed out and hung on the wall. It was clearly some kind of hit list. I don't think the blast ruined too much of it. It could be used against Ace."

"My associates will be taking pictures and any other evidence they can find to build a case against Ace. We might not be official, but we know how to get everything into the officials' hands. Tony being dead makes him the perfect scapegoat for a lot of the stuff that carries the chance at a life sentence, and God knows Ace will use that all he can. Ace will get jail time, he's too connected, but I don't think we're going to get him on murder."

"If we put him away for a while, we can build a bigger case while he's inside," Jamison replied.

"I sure hope you're right, because if you're not, we're all in danger. Serious danger. Worse than it was. Bad enough to escape him. Actually put him in jail? We're targets now. I don't think the kind he'll wait on."

"We'll handle it. Whatever comes, we'll handle it."

Cody looked at where Ace was being shoved into a car. "We may have to kill him yet."

Jamison knew it was possible, but it would also be his last resort. And he wouldn't let his brothers be the ones to live with that weight. "We're better than that. Better than him."

Cody sighed, and he didn't have to say the words for Jamison to know what that sigh meant.

I'm not so sure.

So, Jamison would have to be sure for the both of them—for all of them.

Despite forever and always working so hard to be *good*, Jamison wasn't so sure he was, in fact, good. He'd worried for years that the evil inside his father might take hold of him.

But here they were. Alive. Having helped save some innocent lives. He'd take that as a win for today.

Cody opened the back door of a big, military-grade-looking SUV. Jamison paused, studying his baby brother. He shook his head in awe. "What *are* you involved in?"

Cody smiled wryly. "After this? Nothing."

LIZA DOZED ON the drive to Cody's "medical center," which looked like any run-of-the-mill hunting cabin Liza had ever seen, but was a full-blown medical clinic inside. She practically punched a doctor who tried to check her out before she could see Gigi.

She finally let the doctor examine her while Gigi sat curled up on her lap, talking about the pretty unicorn the lady doctor had given her.

Liza tried not to cry and did a pretty good job of it. Gigi dozed on her lap and Liza let the female doctor—well, Liza assumed she was a doctor—fix her stitches and patch up all her other injuries. They gave her crutches to help stay off her sprained ankle.

"You'll need to take it easy for a few weeks."

Liza laughed. "Yeah, you don't have to tell me twice." She looked down at Gigi, who was fast sleep in her lap. "These girls… Were they…" Liza couldn't bring herself to say it.

"Aside from a few bumps and bruises and a little undernourishment, Gigi is fine. She'll recover in no time."

Liza knew what that meant. "But the others?"

"I can't tell you about the others, Liza. I'm sorry.

Patient confidentiality. I've taken good care of them, and they're safe because of you."

Liza managed a smile for the doctor, though she didn't feel it. It turned out saving someone wasn't the be-all and end-all she'd always assumed it was. She understood Jamison better now, because saving someone meant they'd been through something awful in the first place.

And that you couldn't take it away simply by saving them. There was some guilt even in a happy ending. Maybe if she focused on the happy, the guilt wouldn't be so bad.

Another woman popped her head in the door. "Cody'd like to talk to you, Liza. I can put Gigi to bed."

Liza's grip tightened on Gigi, and the woman smiled warmly. "You're not going to be able to carry her with your ankle. I'll carry her, and show you right where I'm going to put her. You can sit in bed with her until you're satisfied. Cody can wait. Might be good for him."

Liza smiled and nodded even though it was weird that all these strangers knew her name, and Gigi's. The woman was kind and seemed to understand how much Liza wanted to stay with Gigi.

She didn't know any of their names, but she trusted them. Trusted Cody. He'd saved their butts— all of them. She owed him just as much as she owed Jamison.

They wouldn't think of it like that, though. Neither of them. She had to swallow against the wave of emotion. She was out of the Sons, and that meant she got to have some part of that goodness again. Grandma Pauline. The Knights. The Wyatt brothers. Jamison...

They'd all be in her life again. In Gigi's life.

The woman gathered up Gigi, and then waited for Liza to get to her feet and balance on the crutches. She led her into a dark room, but there was a night-light plugged into the wall. There were a variety of beds—some that had clearly been pushed in from other rooms. So the girls could be together.

The woman laid Gigi down on an empty bed, then stepped back so Liza could tuck her in.

Gigi didn't so much as shift or whimper as Liza covered her. Liza sat there for a moment, looking at Gigi's sleeping form, then looking around the room. The sisters slept cuddled together in the same bed, but most of the other girls were in beds of their own. All fast asleep.

They were safe. Maybe they'd seen horrors, but they'd survived them.

The woman nodded toward the door and Liza reluctantly followed her outside.

"We've got a monitor. If anyone wakes up scared, we'll send in either you or one of our people they've been introduced to. We want to make this as easy on them as we can, I promise you."

Liza nodded, afraid she'd start crying if she spoke. She was led to another room. She realized the front of the cabin was deceptive, or it had been in the low light of dawn. It seemed to keep going, farther and farther back. Exam rooms and bedrooms and now this room that reminded Liza of an interrogation room.

But Jamison was there—all sorts of bandages on his face, his arm in a sling. He looked up at her, exhaustion dug into every line on his face.

Love slammed into her so hard and painful, that no matter how well she'd held herself together up until this point, she lost it all here and now.

A sob escaped her mouth, and she was completely immobilized by all of it.

Not even a second went by before Jamison's arms were around her. "Shh. It's all right. We're all right."

She shook her head, feeling stupid and foolish and just wrung out. "Sit down. You're hurt," she croaked, even as she held on to him for dear life.

He rubbed his hand up and down her back and kissed her temple. "I'm fine. I'm fine. Come on, baby. You're killing me. It's all right now."

She leaned into him, letting it all pour out. It *was* all right. No matter what they had to face in the future, they could. They would. Because they'd made this all right, and if they could do that—kill her father, put Ace in jail, stop a human trafficking ring—they could do anything.

She managed to pull herself together, let Jamison lead her to a chair at a table. He nudged her into it, leaned her crutches on the wall, then took the seat next to her. Cody sat on the opposite side of the table, a tablet in front of him.

"I wanted to brief you on the future for the girls," Cody said, all business, as if she hadn't sobbed her guts out in front of him. As if she hadn't known him when he was a baby or a pudgy toddler. "We're checking missing persons files first. But the ones we know for sure are Sons girls… We could find good families for them without going through the state."

"How?" Jamison demanded. "They'll need records and to go to school and—"

Cody smiled at Jamison before he interrupted, "By ways I shouldn't explain in the presence of a by-the-book cop."

Jamison winced at that, but he didn't push Cody for specifics. Cody turned to Liza.

"In your case, Liza, the state would likely award you custody of Gigi through the normal channels. You're the closest living relative that we know about, and Gigi knows you. If you wanted—"

"Of course that's what I want," Liza snapped.

"All right. We'll get you in touch with the right people and make sure it goes as smoothly as possible." Cody's expression changed, though Liza couldn't read it. "You haven't asked about the horse."

Liza winced and shook her head. "I don't want to know. Really, I—"

"I got him out," Jamison interrupted. "I didn't know if he'd get out of the blast zone, but I got him out of the stables."

Liza looked at Jamison in complete awe. He'd somehow saved himself *and* George?

"The rescue team I called out to get the girls found him in the woods. Gigi told him he saved her. So, we got him out, too."

Liza laughed. It was all she could seem to do. They were all safe and whole. Even George the horse.

Unfortunately, no matter how thrilled and relieved she was, there were still serious worries that hadn't been addressed.

"What about Ace?" Liza asked, wishing she could doze on Jamison's lap like Gigi had slept in hers.

"He's currently being held at Pennington County Jail. We're working with local law enforcement on state charges. I've also got one of the men in my group working on what we can get going on the federal level."

Jamison nodded. "Now, most important, when can we go home?"

"When the girls wake up, we'll move you. Grandma and Duke agreed to put up all the girls until we get them placed. We're trying to move as fast on that as we can so they don't feel like they're being juggled, but we don't want to overlook anything. Wherever we place them, it'll be permanent. They'll be taken care of well, and not just now, either. We'll keep tabs. Keep them safe. It's what we do."

Liza rested her head against Jamison's shoulder, beyond tired. "I just want to go home."

Jamison rested his arm over her shoulders, holding her close. "Soon, Liza. Soon."

Chapter Twenty

The ranch was chaos, but the kind that made Jamison smile.

Grandma had taken in four of the girls, including Gigi. Three were over at the Knight ranch, being looked after by Duke—and Sarah and Rachel, his two daughters who still lived on the ranch. And best of all, four of the girls had been placed back with the families they'd been kidnapped from.

Regardless of how many were still staying at the ranches, every night everyone descended on Grandma Pauline's dining room for dinner as they were doing right now.

Four of the girls were being placed in their new homes tomorrow, and the parents who'd agreed to adopt them had come for dinner, too. The house was bursting at the seams, and Grandma ran her kitchen like the general she was.

When they sat down to eat, Duke told stories that had them all laughing. It felt like Christmas. A celebration.

In so many ways, it was. A celebration of survival

and life and knowing they all had futures to build ahead of them.

Once dinner was done, all the girls moved to the stables. It was now a nightly routine for everyone to pet and coo over hero-horse George, whom Cody had managed to transport to the ranch.

He had the much-deserved life of a hero now.

Jamison and whichever brothers were home were relegated to cleanup—he and Cody were currently handling dishes while Dev wiped down the table and swept up the debris before sneaking out to feed the dogs some scraps.

Cody had spent most of the past three days at Grandma's. As if he was planning on staying right here.

"So, when are you going to tell us about this group?" Jamison asked as Cody handed him a plate to dry.

"Never." Cody grinned, but his smile dimmed some and he went back to the dishes he was washing. "Once this is officially over, I'm kicked out."

"Why?"

"Too much connection. It's a secret group, Jamison. I compromised the secret."

"You helped people. You saved us."

Cody paused in his scrubbing for a second, then shook his head. "It's only ever temporary. We know any mission could expose us and we'll have to move on. It's part of the group." Cody shrugged. "I did my time. I helped some people. Now I'll have to figure out what's next. Seems like Dev could use some help around here."

"You hate ranch work."

"Maybe I'll find a new taste for it in my old age."

"You won't." Jamison chuckled, because he realized that Cody might stick around the ranch for a while, but he'd find something else. He'd found this "group" on his own and done good things...whatever they all were. He'd find a way to do more good things, Jamison had no doubt. "You know, you're not so old the police academy would reject you."

"We'll see."

Jamison could have pushed Cody, but there was no need. It wouldn't be a bad idea for his brother to stick around the ranch. They'd need to keep an eye on things these first few months and make sure the Sons didn't band back together stronger without Ace than they'd been with him.

Jamison doubted it, but they still had to be careful.

They finished the dishes, joined the others until they slowly began to disperse. Grandma and Liza put the girls left with them to bed. Cody had disappeared to his room, and Dev and Sarah were out doing the last chores of the evening.

So, Jamison climbed the stairs. His body still wasn't healed—not by a long shot. But he'd get there.

He walked down the hallway to the door to the room Gigi was sleeping in. The door was open, and Liza was curled up in bed with Gigi, telling her a story.

Jamison watched until Liza finished telling Gigi the story. With an elaborate happy ending that Gigi sighed over. Liza handed her the unicorn one of the doctors had given her, then pulled the blanket up to Gigi's chin.

"Stay till I fall asleep, sissy?"

"Always, baby."

Jamison waited. When Liza finally slid away from Gigi's bed, she didn't act surprised to see him in the doorway. She smiled.

She closed the door behind her and they stood in the hallway. The past few nights she'd spent in the same room with Gigi, not wanting to leave her. They hadn't had a chance to really talk.

They had a lot to talk about.

"Where are your crutches?"

"They're more of a pain than this sprain. I'm fine," Liza replied irritably. She gave him an enigmatic sideways look. "How long until you have to go back?"

He frowned in spite of himself. "Desk duty calls." It would bore him to death, truth be told. He might not need to be constantly solving crime, but he liked to be out and active in the community.

And he liked being here, though that had more to do with her and Gigi than anything Bonesteel lacked.

Liza frowned at that. "You're hurt."

"I can take calls. Gage's got my Bonesteel attachment for the time being, which means I absolutely need to go back to work and give him the trouble he's always giving me." He reached out and squeezed her arm. "You'll both be safe here. For as long as you need."

LIZA STARED AT the man she loved, who'd given her the space to all but smother Gigi these past few days. She'd needed that. Some time to focus on Gigi alone. To think about what their new life would look like.

But it didn't look like anything without Jamison in it. He wanted her to stay here. Out of the way and safe. Because he loved her, and he was a man who'd spent his life saving people. So, he thought love was sacrifice.

She'd have to teach him otherwise. She placed her hand on his chest. "I can think of another place we'd be safe."

Jamison stared at her hand, then at her. He looked hurt almost, which didn't make any sense to her.

"Liza…if you want to take Gigi somewhere far away, I'd understand. I could help. But you should wait—"

"I'm not talking about far away," she said, giving him a light shove. "I'm taking about a town with a school, and a very serious police officer keeping the streets safe."

He opened his mouth, but he didn't say anything.

"Unless you're taking back all the love stuff."

He straightened. "I'm not taking back anything."

"Ace is in jail," she said, wrapping her arms around his neck.

"For now," Jamison said, but his arms came around her waist. She could see the worry in him, *feel* it. But he wasn't stepping back.

"Even if he wasn't, I'm on his list." When Jamison

tensed, she kissed his jaw. "You know I am," she said gently.

"What about Gigi?"

"It just so happens I have a great role model in keeping younger siblings safe. She'll be safe with me. With *us*."

"You could both disappear. If you gave me time, I could—"

"For how long?" Liza shook her head. A younger her would have been hurt that he could live without her, but the woman she was now understood all too well he was just trying to protect. "You could have sent your brothers to the ends of the earth. You all could have left. But you stayed, because this is home, and because they dictated too much of our lives already. We stay, Jamison. And if we're in danger, we fight. Together."

"I love you. I want you by my side, Liza, but—"

"No *but*s. That's it. We love each other. We'll keep each other safe. And we'll both do everything in our power to keep Gigi safe and happy. What more could a girl want?"

"Well, probably a better place to live than a shabby, empty apartment above the local lawyer's office."

"So, we'll find a house."

He looked down at her, so serious. If she hadn't always loved him, that careful, serious study would have done it.

"If we find a house, we're going to be finding the altar," he said resolutely, something like a challenge.

She merely raised an eyebrow. "You think that scares me?"

"I don't think anything scares you, Liza. But… Realistically…"

"Realistically I faced death about ten times in the past week."

He brushed a piece of hair away from her face, and when he spoke his voice was gentle. "So, maybe we're not in the best place to be making lifetime commitments."

Liza laughed. She couldn't help it. "How many women have you been with in the past fifteen years?"

He straightened, all flustered and indignant. Adorable and perfect. And hers. Always hers.

"I don't see what that has to do with anything we're talking about."

"Not very many, then."

"I didn't say… That doesn't mean…"

"It means you were waiting for me, whether you admitted it to yourself or not. Because you made a promise to me a long time ago, and you, Jamison Wyatt, don't break promises." She let out a sigh, because it was true now, and it would always be true. "Even when you want to. You were waiting, because somewhere deep down you knew we'd find our way back. Just like I did, no matter how little I could let myself hope for it."

"I don't know how it's possible. To be apart for so long and change in a million ways, and yet… I don't believe in any of that stuff. In knowing what we don't actually know. Waiting without realizing. I don't believe in it. But..."

"Here it is."

"Here it is," he repeated, lowering his mouth to hers. But he didn't kiss her. Not just yet. "I guess it doesn't matter how, as long as we believe it is."

"I do," she said, then pressed her mouth to his instead of waiting for him to get around to it.

Because her future was now, and she'd always been fighting for one with this very good man.

* * * * *

Annalise's heart beat so fast her stomach churned with nausea and an icy chill filled her veins. Bert was dead? The security guard with the great smile who loved to tell silly jokes was gone? And what two women had been killed? Who had been in the office at the time of this... this attack?

What were these killers doing here? What did they want?

The sound of distant sirens pierced the air. The big man cursed loudly.

"We were supposed to get in and out of here before the cops showed up," the tall, thin man said with barely suppressed desperation in his voice.

"Too late for that now," the big man replied. He turned and pointed his gun at Annalise. She stiffened. Was he going to kill her, as well? Was he going to shoot her right now? Kill the girls? She put her arms around her students and tried to pull them all behind her.

More sirens whirred and whooped, coming closer and closer.

"Don't move," he snarled at them. He took the butt of his gun and busted out one of the windows. The sound of the shattering glass followed by a rapid burst of gunfire out the window made her realize just how dangerous this situation was.

The police were outside. She and her students were inside with murderous gunmen, and she couldn't imagine how this all was going to end.

Don't miss
48 Hour Lockdown *by Carla Cassidy,*
available March 2020 wherever
Harlequin Intrigue books and ebooks are sold.

Harlequin.com

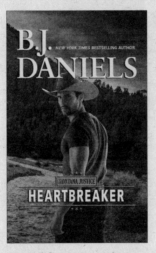

Love Harlequin romance?

DISCOVER.

Be the first to find out about promotions, news and exclusive content!

 Facebook.com/HarlequinBooks

Twitter.com/HarlequinBooks

 Instagram.com/HarlequinBooks

Pinterest.com/HarlequinBooks

ReaderService.com

EXPLORE.

Sign up for the Harlequin e-newsletter and download a free book from any series at **TryHarlequin.com**

CONNECT.

Join our Harlequin community to share your thoughts and connect with other romance readers!
Facebook.com/groups/HarlequinConnection